Barbarians from the Isle

DEDICATION

For Lisa —
may your journeys
always bring you home

With thanks to
the Alberta Foundation
for the Literary Arts
for support through
a research grant.

BARBARIANS FROM THE ISLE

SIGMUND BROUWER

ChariotVICTOR
PUBLISHING
A DIVISION OF COOK COMMUNICATIONS

THE WINDS OF LIGHT SERIES

Wings of an Angel

Barbarians from the Isle

Legend of Burning Water

The Forsaken Crusade

A City of Dreams

Merlin's Destiny

The Jester's Quest

Dance of Darkness

Cover design by Mardelle Ayres
Cover illustration by Jeff Haynie
Photo by Dwight Arthur
Editing by Loreli Dickerson and Lizabeth J. Duckworth

Library of Congress Cataloging-in-Publication Data

Brouwer, Sigmund, 1959–
    Barbarians from the isle / by Sigmund Brouwer.
      p.   cm. — (The Winds of light series: #2)
    Summary: Fourteen-year-old Thomas, lord of Magnus, tries to
thwart a Druid attempt to reconquer his kingdom. Sequel to "Wings
of an Angel."
    ISBN 0-89693-116-1
    [1. Knights and knighthood—Fiction. 2. Civilization, Medieval—
Fiction. 3. Druids and druidism—Fiction. 4. England—Fiction.
5. Christian life—Fiction.] I. Title. II. Series: Brouwer, Sigmund,
1959– Winds of light series: #2.
PZ7.B79984Bar 1992
[Fic]—dc20

    91-40268
    CIP
    AC

Chariot Books is an imprint of ChariotVictor Publishing,
a division of Cook Communications, Colorado Springs, Colorado 80918
Cook Communications, Paris, Ontario
Kingsway Communications, Eastbourne, England

4 5 6 7 8 9 10 Printing/Year 01 00 99 98 97

AUTHOR'S NOTE

For two thousand years—far north and east of London—the ancient English towns of Pickering, Thirsk, and Helmsley, and their castles, have guarded a line on the lowland plains between the larger centers of Scarborough and York.

In the beginning, Scarborough, with its high North Sea cliffs, was a Roman signal post. From there, sentries could easily see approaching barbarian ships, and were able to relay messages from Pickering to Hemsley to Thirsk, the entire fifty miles inland to the boundary outpost of York, where other troops waited—always ready—for any inland invasions.

When their empire fell, the Romans in England succumbed to the Anglo-Saxons, great savage brutes in tribal units who conquered as warriors, and over the generations became farmers. The Anglo-Saxons in turn suffered defeat by raiding Vikings, who in turn lost to the Norman knights from France with their thundering war horses.

Through those hundreds and hundreds of years, that line from Scarborough to York never diminished in importance.

Some of England's greatest and richest abbeys—religious re-
treats for monks, long before the religious Reformation—accu-
mulated their wealth on the lowland plains along that line.
Rievaulx Abbey, just outside Helmsley, contained 270 monks
and owned vast estates of land which held over 13,000 sheep.
But directly north lay the moors.

No towns or abbeys tamed the moors, which reached east
hundreds of square miles to the craggy cliffs of the cold gray
North Sea.

Each treeless and windswept moor plunged into deep divid-
ing valleys of lush greenness that only made the heather-cov-
ered heights appear more harsh. The ancients called these
North York moors "Blackamoor."

Thus, in the medieval age of chivalry, 270 years after the
Norman knights had toppled the English throne, this remote-
ness and isolation protected Blackamoor's earldom of Magnus
from the prying eyes of King Edward II and the rest of his royal
court in London.

Magnus, as a kingdom within a kingdom, was small in com-
parison to the properties of England's greater earls. This small-
ness too was protection. Hard to reach and easy to defend,
British and Scottish kings chose to overlook it, and in practical
terms, it had as much independence as a separate country.

Magnus still had size, however. Its castle commanded and
protected a large village and many vast moors. Each valley between the moors averaged in length a full day's travel by foot.
Atop the moors, great flocks of sheep grazed on the tender
green shoots of heather. The valley interiors supported cattle
and cultivated plots of land, farmed by peasants nearly made
slaves by the yearly tribute exacted from their crops. In short,
with sheep and wool and cattle and land, Magnus was not a
poor earldom, and was well worth ruling.

The entire story of Magnus is difficult to relate in a single volume. *Barbarians from the Isle* begins the portion of its tale which occurs immediately after the orphan boy Thomas—now 14 and in those times old enough to be considered a man—has conquered Magnus and released its village from murderous oppression. (That part of the tale is told in *Wings of an Angel.*)

Magnus itself cannot be found in any history book. Nor can Thomas be found. Nor his nurse Sarah, the wandering knight Sir William, Katherine, Geoffrey the Candlemaker, Tiny John, nor others of the collection of friends and foes of Thomas. Yet many of the more famous people and events found throughout its story shaped the times of that world, as historians may easily confirm.

1

THOMAS
The Valley of Surrender
SUMMER A. D. 1312

Thrust! Thrust! *Slash sideways to parry the counterthrust! Thrust again!*

A small group of hardened soldiers watched impassively as Thomas weakened slowly in defense against their captain.

Ignore the dull ache of fatigue that tempts you to lower your sword hand, Thomas commanded himself. *Advance! Retreat! Quickly thrust! Now parry!*

Above Thomas, gray clouds of a cold June day. Around him, a large area of worn grass, and beyond the dirt and grass, the castle keep and village buildings within the walls of Magnus, the kingdom he had won barely a month earlier.

Right foot forward with right hand. Concentrate. Blink the salt sweat from your eyes. And watch his sword hand!

A small boy struggled to push his way through the wall of soldiers blocking him from Thomas.

He can sense you weakening. He pushes harder. You cannot fight much longer. Formulate a plan!

"Thomas!" the boy cried. One burly soldier clamped a massive hand around the boy's arm and held him back.

Thomas began to gasp for air in great ragged gulps. His sword drooped. His quick steps blurred in precision.

The captain, a full hand taller than Thomas, grinned.

The death thrust comes soon! Lower your guard now!

Thomas flailed tiredly and relaxed one moment too long.

His opponent stretched his grin wider, and—overconfident because of the obvious fatigue in front of him—brought his sword high to end the fight.

Now!

Thomas focused all his remaining energy on swinging his sword beneath that briefly unguarded upstroke. The impact of sword on ribs jarred his arm to the elbow. He danced back, expecting victory.

Instead, the captain roared with rage as he fell backward onto the dirt and scrabbled to his feet.

"Insolent puppy! Now learn your lesson!"

Among the soldiers, a few faces showed amusement. The small boy now held among them kicked his captor in the shins, but could not free himself.

The captain rushed forward and waved his sword.

Intent on saving what energy he could, Thomas merely held his own sword carefully in front to guard. He watched the waving sword as a mouse in hiding watches a cat.

"Fool!" the captain shouted, still waving the sword in his right hand as distraction while his left hand flew upward in an arc that Thomas barely saw. At the top of that arc, the captain released a fistful of loose dirt into the eyes and mouth of his younger opponent.

Thomas caught most of the dirt as he sucked in a lungful of air. The rest blinded him with pain. The choking retch forced Thomas to his knees, as if in prayer, and he did not see the captain's sword flash downward.

Once across the side of the ribs. Then a symbolic point thrust in the center of his chest.

Over.

The soldiers hooted and clapped, before dispersing to their daily duties. The small boy broke loose as his captor joined the applause. He darted to Thomas.

"That dirt was an unfair thing for 'im to do, it was!" the boy said.

In reply, Thomas coughed twice more, then staggered to his feet.

"Wooden swords and protective horsehide vests or not, my lord," the captain said to Thomas, "I expect you'll be taking a few bruises to your bed tonight."

Thomas spit dirt from his mouth. "I expect you'll have one yourself, Robert. It was no light blow I dealt to your ribs. By our rules, I thought the fight would end." He wiped his face and left a great smudge of sweat-oiled dirt.

The boy tugged on his sleeve. "Thomas."

"Later, Tiny John."

"Rightfully so. By our rules, you *were* the winner," Robert of Uleran replied. He was a man, at thirty years old, nearly middle aged. Solid and tough, his scarred and broken face was a testimony to much of the first three decades of rough living. Set in anger, children would run from that face screaming. But when he smiled, as he did now, no child would ever be frightened.

"I continued, however, for two reasons," Robert of Uleran said.

Thomas spit more dirt from his mouth and waited.

"One, I was angry you had fooled me by pretending tiredness so effectively. A teacher should never misjudge his student so badly. It's been a month and you've learned far quicker than most. I should have expected that move from you."

"Thomas!" Tiny John said.

"Later, Tiny John." Then, attention back to Robert of Uleran. "Anger has never been part of the rules," Thomas observed.

"Neither has mercy. And do ιοτ deny it." Robert's eyes flashed beneath thick dark eyebrows. "When you landed that first blow, you should have moved in to finish me. Instead, you paused. That hesitation may cost you your life someday."

Robert drew his cloak aside and began to unbind the thick horse leather wrapped around his upper body for protection. "I will not impart to you all I know about fighting only to have you lose to a lesser man with more cruelty. The dirt in your face, I hope, has proved to be a great lesson."

"Thomas!" Tiny John blurted, then stamped his feet in frustration and rolled his eyes in exasperation.

Thomas good-naturedly placed a hand over Tiny John's mouth. He knew this was the proper time to make his announcement.

"Robert," he said, "I do not wish for you to remain captain of all these soldiers. Pick your replacement."

Robert of Uleran stared in disbelief. "My lord, have I offended you?"

"Pick your replacement," Thomas ordered. Thomas was already in his fourteenth year, nearly a man, and certainly a man in action. As Lord of Magnus, he could not allow anyone to question him lightly.

"Yes, my lord."

Tiny John considered biting the hand over his mouth. But even he recognized the steel in Thomas' voice, and decided there would be a better time later.

"David of Fenway, my lord," Robert said. "He shows great promise and the men respect him."

Having said that, Robert of Uleran turned. He had not completed the removal of his fighting gear. Yet because of angry pride, he turned to leave quickly.

"Please remove your possessions from the soldier's quarters," Thomas ordered.

For a moment, Robert's face expanded with rage at the further insult. His narrow scar lines flushed with blood, and he drew a deep breath. He wheeled quickly and stared at Thomas. Neither flinched.

Then Robert's shoulders sagged. "Yes, my lord."

Thomas drew his own breath to speak, but was interrupted by the drumming of horse hooves.

A great white beast rounded the buildings opposite the exercise area. On it, a man in a flowing purple cape. Sword sheathed in scabbard. No travel bags attached to the saddle.

Thomas removed his hand from Tiny John's face, and placed it on Robert's shoulder to stop him from moving away.

"It's the Earl of York," Tiny John blurted. "That's what I was trying to tell you. The most powerful man in the land! He asked permission at the gates to enter alone and unguarded. Twenty of his men remain outside."

The Earl of York! Magnus, tucked in the remotest valley of the North York moors, still lay within jurisdiction of the Earl of York. Thomas had known it was only a matter of time until he faced his next challenge as new Lord of Magnus. *Would the earl accept a new loyalty pact? Or was he here to declare war?*

The horse arrived within moments, and the man dismounted with an easy grace.

He immediately moved forward to Robert of Uleran and extended his right hand to show it bare of weapons. "Thomas of Magnus. I am David Hawkley, Earl of York."

Robert was in no mood to enjoy the mistake. "The Lord of Magnus stands beside me."

The earl's eyes widened briefly with surprise. He recovered quickly and extended his right hand to Thomas.

"I come in peace," he said. "I beg of you to receive me in equal manner."

"We shall extend to you the greatest possible hospitality," Thomas answered. "And I wish for you to greet Robert of

Uleran, the man I trust most within Magnus, and . . ." Thomas paused to enjoy the announcement he had been about to make—"newly appointed sheriff of this manor. He may be busy, however, over the next few hours as he moves his possessions to his new residence in the keep."

If the Earl of York did not understand the reason for Robert's sudden and broad smile of happiness, he was polite enough not to ask.

Thomas, with Robert, led the Earl of York and his horse to the stables. There, he summoned a boy to tend to the horse.

It took great willpower not to bombard the air with questions. Thomas, however, remembered advice that he had been given by an old friend, now dead. *The one who speaks first shows anxiousness, and in so doing, loses ground.*

Instead, Thomas contented himself with a very ordinary observation. "The clouds promise rain," he said as they left the shelter of the stables.

The Earl of York looked up from his study of the nearby archery practice range. "I fear much more than rain."

Thomas waited, but the earl said nothing more until their walk brought them to the keep of Magnus.

"A moat within the castle walls?" he asked.

In front of them lay a shallow ditch. *Had it only been four weeks since Thomas had filled it with tar and crackling dry wood and threatened to siege the former lord and his soldiers unless they gave up without bloodshed?*

"Temporary," Thomas commented, and volunteered no further information.

The earl paused and looked upward at the keep. Four stories high and constructed of stone walls more than three feet thick, it was easily the most imposing structure within the walls of Magnus. Not even the cathedral compared in magnificence.

Thomas too gazed in appreciation. From the top turrets, he often surveyed the lake that surrounded the castle walls and stared deep in thought at the high steep hills of the moors which were etched against the sky. Morning was best, before the wind began and when the heather—that endless low carpet of brush—glowed purple in the sun's first rays.

From these turrets, early each morning Thomas turned and watched Magnus itself as it began to stir. There was the street of shops, each with a large painted sign to show its trade in symbol—for few people could read. Then curved the narrow streets with houses so cramped together and leaning in all directions that they were like crooked dirty teeth.

And of course, the cathedral. Thomas would smile to turn his eyes upon the steeple that rose from the depths of the village. Not because of the priest. No, as an orphan, Thomas had been mistreated by corrupt monks and had decided to hate religion. He smiled instead because of an old man given the task of sweeping the stone floors there, an old man named Gervase who Thomas had once confused for the priest, an old man who truly believed in the God that Thomas struggled to find, and who seemed to live in a manner which showed belief. Not like priests and monks who preyed upon the poor and innocent.

Thomas almost growled at that thought, then stopped. He was, after all, standing beside the Earl of York, the most powerful man for hundreds of miles in any direction.

He glanced at the earl to see if he too had finished his inspection of the keep. The earl nodded.

Thomas almost smiled at the demonstration of power. *Subtle. This man appearing to give me permission to allow him to enter my hall.*

They climbed the outside steps with Robert following. Tiny

John, always easily bored, had scampered away from them into the village.

The entrance to the keep was twenty feet from the ground, designed that way to make it difficult for attackers to gain entrance.

The ground level—which they would have to reach by descending an inside stairway, contained the food stores and the kitchen on one side, and the open hall for eating and entertainment to the middle and rest of the other side.

Above—the keep was designed in a large square—were the three residential stories, with the lord's rooms on the top. Each level was open in the center and looked down upon the hall, so that all rooms were tucked against the four outer walls. Below, only reached by a narrow passageway, was the dungeon, deep enough below the stone that cries of prisoners would never reach the hall.

Thomas always shuddered to think of that hole of endless night. He had spent much too long there once, almost doomed before he could even start the events which led to his conquering Magnus. And now—the thought was always on his mind, even as he swung open the great doors of the keep to allow inside the Earl of York—the dungeon held two silent and cowed prisoners who were proving to be his thorniest problems as a new lord.

Until the arrival of the earl.

"I shall leave, my lord?" Robert asked.

"As you wish," Thomas said. He would have appreciated the man beside him during a discussion with the earl. But the need for help might show weakness. Thomas was glad that Robert knew it too. It said much for the man's thinking.

Thomas gestured at two leather padded chairs near the hearth. Before they had time to sit, a maid appeared with a steaming mixture of milk, sugar, and crushed barley.

"No wine?" The earl raised an eyebrow.

Did that mean scorn?

Thomas remembered the instructions from the friend of long ago. *Never show fear. Nor hesitation.*

"No wine. It tends to encourage sloth."

The earl grinned. "There's gentle criticism if I ever heard it. And from someone so young."

They studied each other.

Thomas, unlike many of the men in Magnus, had kept his hair long. Tied back, it seemed to add strength to the impression already given by square shoulders, a high intelligent forehead, a straight noble nose, and an untrembling chin.

Young Thomas had good reason to be frightened. The Earl of York had shown much strength by entering his castle alone. Thomas knew the earl held almost as much power as the King of Britain himself. Yet he forced himself to appear calm, willing his gray eyes not to betray him.

Thomas repeated to himself, *Never show fear. Nor hesitation.* He wanted to close his eyes briefly to silently thank Sarah, the one who had spent many hours drilling him on how to act. She and she alone had believed he would someday rule Magnus. And now he faced his first great test. *What does the earl want? What is he thinking?*

The earl looked as if he did not know whether to frown or laugh as the silence grew.

Thomas lifted his thick ceramic cup in a wordless salute. The earl responded in turn and gulped the thick, sweet broth.

Still Thomas waited for the earl to break and utter the first words.

His eyes did not leave the earl's face. Thomas saw a man already forty years old, but with a face quite different than one would expect of royalty at that age. The chin had not doubled, or tripled, with good living. There were no broken veins on his nose to suggest too much enjoyment of wine. No sagging circles beneath his eyes betrayed sleepless nights from poor health or a bad conscience.

Instead, the face was broad and remarkably smooth. Neatly trimmed red-blond hair spoke of Vikings among his ancestors. His blue eyes matched the sky just before dusk. Straight, strong teeth now gleamed in a smile.

"Do you treat all visitors this harshly?" the earl asked.

"Sir! I beg of you forgiveness. Do you wish to dine immediately?"

"It is hardly the food, or lack thereof. Surely you have questions, yet you force me to begin!"

"Again, I beg of you forgiveness."

"If you want me to believe that, you have to stop hiding that smile." The earl laughed at the discomfort he produced with that statement. "Enough," he then said, "I see you and I shall get along famously. I detest men who offer me their throats like craven dogs."

"Thank you, my lord," Thomas said quietly. He coughed. "I presume you are here to inspect me."

The earl nodded.

"I thought as much," Thomas said. "Otherwise you would not have made such a show of mistakenly greeting my sheriff, Robert."

This time, the earl had enough grace to show discomfort. "My acting was so poor?"

Thomas shook his head. "Only a fool would have entered Magnus without knowing anything about his future ally—or opponent. Between Robert and I, you should have easily guessed which one was young enough to be the new Lord of Magnus."

Thomas held his breath.

Yet the Earl of York decided to let the reference to ally or opponent slip past them both. He sipped again from his broth.

"Do your men practice their archery often?"

"With all due respect, my lord," Thomas answered, "I think you mean to question me about the distance between the men and their targets."

This time, the earl did not bother to hide surprise.

"You are a man of observation," Thomas said simply. "And a fighting man. I saw your eyes measure the ground from where the grass was trampled to where the targets stand. I would guess a man with experience in fighting would think it senseless to have practice at such great distance."

"Yes," the earl said. "I had wondered. But I had also reserved judgment."

"I am having the men experiment with new bows."

"New bows? How so?"

Thomas showed that the question had been indiscreet by ignoring it. "In so doing, I also wish to let them understand it is my main desire that they survive battles. Not die gloriously. Distance between battle lines ensures that."

The earl took his rebuke with a calm nod. "Truly, that is a remarkable philosophy in this age."

Thomas did not tell the earl it was a strategy already 1,400 years old, a strategy from a far land, and a strategy contained in the books of knowledge hidden from here, which had enabled him to conquer Magnus.

"Not one soldier died as Magnus fell," Thomas said instead. "That made it much easier to obtain loyalty from a fighting force."

"You have studied warfare?" The earl did not hide his amazement.

"In a certain manner, yes." Thomas also decided it would be wiser to hide that not only could he read—a rarity in itself and mostly restricted to the higher ranked priests or monks—but could read and speak French, the language of the nobles, and English and Latin.

The Earl of York decided to follow a hunch. Everything told him that Thomas showed great promise.

He told Thomas so. "When I arrived," he continued, "I had not decided what I might do about your new status. I feared I might be forced to waste time by gathering a full force and laying a dreadfully long siege. Please know that I will not."

"Again, I thank you."

"You may not," the earl said heavily.

Thomas raised an eyebrow to imply a question.

"Because of what my heart believes," the earl said, "I wish to seal with you a loyalty pact. You may remain lord here with my full blessing."

Thomas hid his joy. A siege, a protracted war would not occur!

"That sounds like a reason for celebration, not concern," Thomas said carefully.

The earl pursed his lips, shook his head slowly, and spoke with regret. "I am here to request you go north and defeat the approaching Scots."

3

"**Come with me,**" the earl said, holding up a thick, strong hand to cut Thomas short as he drew a breath. "We shall walk throughout your village."

Thomas, still stunned, managed a weak smile. *At least the earl calls it my village.*

They retraced their steps back through the keep, and remained alone.

Within minutes, the crowded and hectic action of the village market swallowed them. Pigs squealed. Donkeys brayed in protest against overloaded carts digging into soft ground. Men shouted. Women shouted. Smells—from the yeasty warmth of baking bread to the pungent filth of emptied chamber pots—swirled around Thomas and the earl.

Despite the push and shove of the crowd, they walked untouched, their rich purple robes badges of authority. People parted a path in front of them, as water does for a ship's bow.

"This battle . . ."

"Not yet." The earl held a finger to his lips.

They walked.

Through the market. Past the church in the center of the village. Past the collections of houses, some whitewashed, some showing decades of dirt.

Finally, at the base of the ramparts farthest from the keep, the Earl of York slowed his stride.

"Here," he said. He pointed back at the keep. "Walls tend to have ears."

Thomas hoped his face had found calmness by then. "You are asking me to risk my newly acquired lordship by leaving Magnus immediately for battle?"

"You have no one you can trust here in your absence?"

"Can anyone be trusted with such wealth at stake?" Thomas answered.

The earl shrugged. "It is a risk placed upon all of us. I too am merely responding to the orders of King Edward the Second." Darkness crossed his face. "I pray my request need not become an order. Nor an order resisted. Sieges are dreadful matters."

Unexpectedly, Thomas grinned.

It startled the earl to see that response to his scowl of power, a scowl which often made grown men flinch.

"That is a well spoken threat." Thomas continued his grin. "A siege of Magnus, as history has proven, is a dreadful matter for *both* sides."

"True enough," the earl admitted. He thoughtfully steepled his fingers below his chin. "But Magnus cannot fight forever."

Sunlight glinted from a huge gold ring. Thomas froze.

The ring! Its symbol matched that of those belonging to both prisoners in the dungeon.

The earl did not realize, of course, the ring's effect. He simply kept speaking as Thomas tried to maintain composure.

"This request for help in battle comes for a twofold reason," the earl said. "First, as you know, earldoms are granted and permitted by order of the King of England, Edward II, may he reign long. The power he has granted me lets me in turn hold sway over the lesser earldoms of the north."

Force yourself to concentrate on conversation. "Earls may choose to rebel," Thomas said.

Another scowl across the Earl of York's wide features. "It has happened before. But those earls are fools. The king can suffer no traitors. He brings to bear upon them his entire fighting force. Otherwise, further rebellion by others is encouraged. You have—rightly or wrongly—gained power within Magnus. You will keep it as long as you swear loyalty to me, which means loyalty to the king."

Thomas nodded. That childhood friend and tutor—the one who had given him the plan to conquer Magnus—had long ago anticipated this and explained. *But did loyalty include joining forces with one who carried the strange symbol?*

Once again, Thomas forced himself to stay in the conversation. "Loyalty, of course, dictates tribute be rendered to you."

"Tribute consists of both goods and, when needed, military support, which I in turn pledge to King Edward," the earl said. "Magnus is yours, that I have already promised. Your price to me is my price to the king. We both must join King Edward in his fight against the Scots."

Thomas knew barely thirty years had passed since King Edward's father had defeated the stubborn tribal Welsh in their rugged hills to the south and east. The Scots to the north, however, had proven more difficult, a task given to Edward II on his father's death. The Scots had a new leader, Robert Bruce, whose counterattacks grew increasingly devastating to the English.

Reasons for battle were convincing, as the earl quickly outlined. "If we do not stop this march by our northern enemies, England may have a new monarch—one who will choose from among *his* supporters many new earls to fill the English estates. Including ours."

Thomas nodded to show understanding. Yet behind that nod, a single thought transfixed him. *The symbol. It belonged to an unseen, unknown enemy. One that the prisoners in the dungeon refused to reveal.*

"Couriers have brought news of a gathering of Scots," the earl explained. "Their main army will go southward on a path near the eastern coast. That army is not our responsibility. A smaller army, however, wishes to take the strategic North Sea castle at Scarborough, only thirty miles from here. I have been ordered to stop it at all costs."

Thomas thought quickly, remembering what he had learned of the North York moors and its geography. "Much better to stop them before they reach the cliffs along the sea."

The earl's eyes widened briefly in surprise. "Yes. A battle along the lowland plains north of here."

"However—"

"There can be no 'however,' " the earl interrupted.

Thomas too could match the earl in coldness. "However," he repeated, flint-toned, "how can I know that this is not merely a ploy to get my army away from this fortress, where we are vulnerable to *your* attack?"

The earl sighed. "I thought you might consider that. As is custom, I will leave in Magnus a son as hostage. I have no need of more wealth, and his life is worth more than twenty earldoms. Keep him here to be killed at the first sign of my treachery."

Thomas closed his eyes briefly in relief. The earl was not lying.

Uncontested by reigning royalty, and given officially by charter, Magnus would now remain his. *If he survived the battle against the Scots. If he survived the mystery behind the symbol on the ring.*

4

By this time tomorrow, I will be committed to war.

Despite the thrill of fear that arrived with the thought, Thomas felt a shiver of joy.

Action, again.

The Earl of York had departed with his twenty men to the main battlecamp—a half day's ride east—to a valley adjoining the territory of Magnus. Thomas now paced in the privacy of his room on the highest floor of the castle keep.

Action. Again.

Every morning, for seven years, Thomas as an orphan in a faraway abbey had woken to one thought—*conquer Magnus.* His childhood nurse and teacher, the only person to show him love, had before her death given him the knowledge to conquer the mighty kingdom. And a reason to do it.

Every night for seven years, the same thought had been his last before entering sleep—*conquer Magnus.*

Yet, strangely, after succeeding in a way that had mesmerized an entire kingdom, Thomas did not feel complete. Was it the

need for action, or an emptiness caused by the loss of the two
friends who had made it possible for him to become lord?

Action. Again.

And another thrill of fear and a shiver of joy. Yet, unlike the
battle of Magnus a month ago, it would be impossible for war
against the Scots to succeed without a single loss of life. *Would
Thomas be numbered among the dead? Or alive, would he see through
the fog that seemed to surround the strange symbol of evil that the Earl
of York had displayed on a ring of gold?*

Thomas clenched his jaw with new determination. One answer, he suddenly realized, might wait for him in the dungeon.
He reached it a few minutes later.

"Our prisoners fare well?" Thomas asked the soldier guarding
the dank passageway to the cells.

"As well as can be expected. Each day, an hour of sunshine
each. But they are never allowed out together." The guard's
voice held faint disapproval at such kind treatment.

*A proper earl would discipline a guard who—even in tone—ques-
tioned orders.*

Thomas smiled instead. "Tell me, I pray, who is crueler? The
oppressor, or the oppressed people who, when finally free, pun-
ish the oppressor with equal cruelty?"

The guard blinked, a movement barely seen in the dim light
of smoky torches. "The oppressor, my lord. 'Tis plain to see."

"Is it plain?" Thoughtfulness filled Thomas' voice. "The oppressor, cruel as he may be, cannot feel the effects of his methods. The oppressed, however, know full well the pain of cruelty.
To give the same in return, knowing its evilness, strikes me as
crueler."

Slow understanding crossed the guard's face. "Your own time
in the dungeon . . ."

"Yes," Thomas said. "You will continue, of course, to ensure a
fresh bedding of straw each day?"

"Certainly, my lord." This time the guard's voice reflected full approval.

Thomas waited for his eyes to adjust to the hazy torch light beyond the guard. He then continued behind the guard through the narrow passageway.

The same rustling of bold rats, the same feeling of cold air that clung damply. Thomas hated the dungeon, hated the need to use it.

There were four cells, iron-barred doors all facing each other. Two held prisoners. A girl, nearly woman, in one. A candlemaker who had tried murdering her in the other.

Thomas ignored the instructions directed by his heart, and strode past the cell which held the girl.

"I wish to see the candlemaker," he told the guard.

The clanking of keys, and the screech of a wooden door protesting on ancient hinges.

"Wait outside," Thomas said as he stepped into the cell. He felt the same despair he did each day to face the prisoner inside. *So much to know, so little given.*

Thomas again asked himself the questions which had haunted him since conquering Magnus.

An old man once cast the sun into darkness and directed me here from the gallows where a knight was about to die, falsely accused. The old man knew Isabelle was a spy, the old man knew my dream of conquering Magnus. Who was that old man? How did he know? Will he ever reappear?

A valiant and scarred knight befriended me and helped me win the castle that once belonged to his own lord. Then he departed. Why?

A crooked candlemaker and Isabelle, the daughter of the lord we vanquished, remain in the dungeons of Magnus, refusing to speak.

What conspiracy had Isabelle been ready to reveal before her near death?

And what fate has fallen upon the other girl, Katherine, whose face is horribly scarred beyond repair, and whose heart of goodness helped me win Magnus?

There are the books filled with priceless knowledge, able to give a young man the power to conquer kingdoms. How will I bring them safely to the castle?

And what are the secrets of Magnus?

The early rays of sun which warmed Thomas on the eastern ramparts had never replied to these silent questions.

The man who might know, Geoffrey the candlemaker, now sat against the far wall, chained to the rough stone blocks. He was a tiny man, with tiny rounded shoulders and a wrinkled compact face. His cheeks bunched into tight apples as he grinned mockery at his visitor.

Thomas did not waste a moment in greeting. "Answer truth, and you shall be free to leave this cell."

The mocking grin only became wider.

Thomas began his usual questions. "Why do you and the girl Isabelle share the strange symbol?"

The usual reply. Nothing.

"She spoke of a conspiracy before you attempted to stop her through death," Thomas continued. "Who conspires and what hold do they have upon you to keep you in silence?"

Only the dripping of condensed water from the ceiling of the cell broke the silence which always followed a question from Thomas.

The test, Thomas told himself. *Now.*

"Your answers no longer matter," Thomas shrugged. "Just today, I have pledged loyalty to the Earl of York."

Watch carefully. Will this man betray allegiance to the same Earl of York?

Geoffrey laughed. The last reaction Thomas had expected. Yet a reaction to give hope. *Either the Earl of York did not belong to those who held the symbol, or the candlemaker excelled as an actor.*

"The earl has as little hope as do you when already the forces of darkness gather to reconquer Magnus," Geoffrey snorted. "You are fools to think Magnus will not return to . . ."

The candlemaker snapped his mouth shut.

"To . . . ?" Thomas pressed. It was as much progress as he had made in the month since capturing Magnus.

That mocking grin shone again in the flickering light. "To those of the symbol," Geoffrey said flatly. "You shall be long dead by their hands, however, before those behind it are revealed to the world."

5

Thomas stood at the rear of the cathedral in the center of Magnus. Late afternoon sun warmed the burnished wood pews and etched shadows into the depths of the curved stone ceiling above.

He waited until the man approached near enough to hear him speak softly.

"Father, I leave tomorrow. I wish to bid farewell."

That was the joke they shared. Thomas always addressed Gervase, the elderly man, as a priest, though he was not.

Instead, the elderly man with gray hair combed straight back served the church as a custodian. As Thomas often remembered, once during anguish of doubt and uncertainty shortly after conquering Magnus, he had finally broken a vow to reject God and the men who served Him. That morning, he had entered the church and mistaken Gervase for a priest.

The questions Thomas had asked that morning, and the answers which Gervase had provided in return, proved a strange but enjoyable beginning for a friendship between a lord and the man who swept the floors of the cathedral.

"Yes," Gervase nodded. "You will lead the men of Magnus into battle against the Scots."

"The procession leaves at dawn—" Thomas stopped himself then blurted, "How is it you knew?"

Gervase laughed. His rich voice matched the strong lines of humor that marked his old skin. His eyes had prompted Thomas to immediate trust their first morning, for they held nothing of the greed too often seen in priests and monks.

"Thomas, you should not be amazed to discover men find it crucial to put their souls in order before any battle. I have seen a great number enter the church today for confessions. Many whom I haven't seen in months."

Not for the first time did Thomas wonder at the educated manner of the older man's speech. Why would someone of his obvious intelligence settle for a lifetime of simple duties?

Gervase saw that doubt flash across the younger man's face, and mistook it for something else. "Again," he chided with a wry smile. "The disbelief. Simple as these men may be at times, they have the wisdom to acknowledge God. Someday, Thomas, the angels will much rejoice to welcome you to the fold."

Thomas said, "I am not convinced there are angels."

The wry smile curved farther upward in response. "Despite the legend you so aptly fulfilled the night you conquered Magnus? *'Delivered on the wings of an angel, he shall free us from oppression.'* I shall never forget the power of that chant, Thomas. The entire population gathered beneath torchlight by the instructions of a single knight. The appearance of a miracle on white angel wings. Yet you yourself doubt angels?"

"Gervase!" Thomas tried to inject anger into his voice. And failed.

"Tomorrow you'll be gone, Thomas. Have you any other miracles to astound the Scots?"

"Gervase! Are you suggesting *I* arranged the miracle of angel wings?"

"Of course. Our Heavenly Father has no need to stoop to such low dramatics."

Thomas sighed. "You would be kind to keep that belief to yourself. As it is, I am able to hold much sway over the rest of Magnus, despite my youth. Leaving this soon would be much less safe for me were it otherwise. I *do* want to be welcomed back as rightful lord."

"*Rightful?* This is indeed news. Has it to do with a certain visitor who entered Magnus earlier in the day?"

"Little escapes you," Thomas commented, then explained much of his conversation with the earl. But Thomas did not mention the symbol, or his fear of it. Some secrets could not be shared.

Gervase listened carefully. When Thomas finished, he spoke with simple grace. "And your prisoners, my friend? Any progress there? Has Geoffrey revealed who instructed him to attempt to murder the former lord's daughter?"

Thomas shook his head. He could not escape the ache which hit him to be reminded of the other prisoner. One who had loved, then betrayed him, almost at the cost of his life.

"Time will answer all," Gervase said. "It was kind of you to visit during a day which demands many preparations."

"I could not have considered otherwise," Thomas replied. The truth in his words surprised him.

Gervase walked with Thomas to the cathedral doors. "I shall continue praying for you, Thomas. The angels *will* rejoice when you accept His most holy presence in your life."

Thomas almost nodded. *Yet how could he believe what he did not see?*

6

Thomas faced his first challenge before the entire army had assembled in the valley.

Council of War had been called. Gathered in a small circle beneath the shade of a towering oak stood fourteen of the most powerful earls and barons—ranked lesser and greater among themselves—in the north. Among them, Thomas.

"David, will you permit such a puppy to remain with us in council?" The questioner, a fat middle-aged man whose chubby fingers were studded with massive gold rings, did not hide his contempt and surprise to see Thomas.

"Aye, Frederick, the puppy remains," replied the Earl of York.

"But these are matters of war!" exploded the fat man, spraying spittle on those nearest him.

Some nodded agreement. Others waited for David Hawkley, the Earl of York, to respond again. All stared at Thomas.

Around these men of power—hundreds upon hundreds of yards in all directions—the army swelled and grew as men marched in from all directions.

Huge war-horses, clothed in fighting colors, stood patiently, attended by anxious squires. Knights, dressed only in tights and light chain mail, rested in shade; mules and servants would carry the heavy armor and swords and lances to the battle site.

The bulk of the army, however, did not consist of expensive battlehorses and pampered, well-trained knights. Instead, it was formed by the men of farms and villages who owed the knights and lords and earls and barons a set number of days of military service each year.

Many were poorly equipped and carried only crude leather shields and sturdy sharpened wooden poles called pikes. These men would form stationary front lines of battle—almost like temporary palisades or walled barriers—while the faster moving knights would charge ahead or retreat on their battlehorses, according to command.

More ably equipped than pikesmen were the yeomen, armed with longbows and capable of raining arrows far beyond the opposing front lines with devastating effect. Most lords set aside a practice range within castle walls and demanded regular archery practice from all men over the age of sixteen.

Others carried crossbows, which fired short bolts with enough fury to pierce even a knight's armor. Crossbows were expensive, however, and difficult to reload. Even strong men were forced to brace the bow in their feet and draw the string back with the full strength of both arms. The less expensive longbows, on the other hand, could be reloaded almost instantly—some men could fire two arrows per second. With the much longer arrow length, longbows were also more accurate than a crossbow.

Thomas' own army held six fully equipped knights—a reflection of the moderate wealth of Magnus, since many earls with more property could only support two or three knights. Each war-horse alone was worth five years' wages; each set of armor, two years' wages; and each knight, nearly the ransom worthy of a king. As superb fighting machines, knights were held loyal by the reward of estates—much of the outlying valleys of Magnus had been given for that purpose.

His army also held ten men with crossbows, and another forty with longbows. His remaining men, all villagers and farmers with wives and large families, were pikesmen who already sweated with fear this far from the lowland plains of future battle.

Most of the earls and barons around Thomas beneath the oak tree had contributed larger armies. The sum of all their armies made for the noise and confusion of thousands of fighting men, plus an almost matching number of cooks and servants and hangers-on. With banners and flags of fighting colors waving like a field of flowers, and the constant movement of people, the gathering around this council of war gave the center of the valley a carnival-like atmosphere.

Part of his mind noted the festive hum beyond the circle of barons, but despite the malice of the fat man in front of Thomas, another part of his thoughts also held sadness—*Before the army's return, many men will die, to leave behind widows and orphans.*

The fat man yelled to repeat his challenge. "These are matters of war!"

Thomas surveyed the other men in the circle. His only friend—if someone carrying the symbol could be a friend—might be David, the Earl of York.

Show no fear. Lose respect here and your own men will never follow. Lose your men, and you lose control of Magnus.

Thomas fought the impulse to lick his suddenly dry lips. If the Earl of York did not vouch for him, he would be forced to prove himself immediately. A fight perhaps. These were solid, grown men, who had clawed for power on the strength of steel nerves and iron willpower. Would Robert of Uleran's training be enough to overcome them?

The Earl of York delayed the answer to that question by replying with the quietness of authority. "Frederick, this 'puppy' you so casually address had the intelligence to conquer alone the ultimate fortress, Magnus itself. Could *you* have done the same, even with an army of a thousand?"

But no, Thomas wanted to protest, Magnus was given me by the power of a hidden treasure, by a long dead nurse and the knowledge of a legend, by a single knight who thought he was riding into certain death, by the winds of the moors . . . and perhaps by the God I was trying to escape.

The Earl of York laughed to break the discomfort of his rebuke. "Besides, Frederick, this 'puppy' is taller than you already. When he fills to match the size of his hands, he'll be a terrible enemy. Treat him well while you can."

The others joined in the laughter.

Thomas realized that if this meeting were to end now, he would simply be regarded as a special pet, favored by the Earl of York. Yet could he risk the earl's anger?

The laughter continued.

"I need no special treatment," Thomas suddenly declared, then felt the thud of his heart in the immediate silence.

Was it too early to reveal the weapons his men had practiced in secrecy?

Thomas hoped the narrowing of the Earl of York's eyes meant curiosity.

You've gone too far to turn back. "Tomorrow, when we rest at midday," Thomas said, "I propose a contest."

7

It took the remainder of the day for all the stragglers to gather. By dusk, the valley seemed entirely full of men and horses.

As Thomas stood in the growing dusk and watched the countless campfires begin to tremble their light, he felt a hand on his shoulder.

"Friend or foe?" Thomas asked with a laugh.

The Earl of York's voice sounded from behind him. "Friend. Most assuredly a friend. And one surprised to hear humor from so serious a man."

There it was again. "Man." Thomas knew it was easier to pretend the role than to be it. Growing older meant showing a confidence he sometimes did not feel. He was glad the earl could not read his doubts or confusions.

While that flashed through his mind, Thomas spoke with a grin. "All you and I have discussed is war. It's hard to find humor in the killing of men."

"Spoken well, Thomas," the earl said. "And I'm here to offer apology. You were indeed right to earlier cast aside my vouch

for you. I may think of you as an equal, but others choose only
to believe what their eyes see, not what is beyond, such as a
man's courage or intelligence."

Thomas barely heard the rest of the earl's encouraging words.

Others choose only to believe what their eyes will see, Gervase had
said . . . *Must God follow Thomas even among the camps of war?*

Dawn broke clear and bright. Despite the cold which resulted
from a cloudless night, few complained. Any rain would be
churned into a sucking mud beneath the thousands of feet of an
army this size. White mist, common to the moors, would disori-
ent stragglers within minutes. Cold and clear nights, then, were
much better for warfare.

Before the sun grew hot, all tents had been dismantled and
packed. Then, with much confusion and shouting, the earls and
barons directed their men so that the entire army formed an
uneven column nearly a half mile in length, and so long that the
front banners began forward motion nearly twenty minutes before the ones in the rear.

The army only marched for three miles before an eerie noise
began.

To Thomas, it sounded like the faraway buzzing of bees—he
once actually lifted his head to search for the cloud of insects.
The whispering became a hum, and the hum gradually became
a babble. *The noise came from the men and women of the army itself.*

Still, the army moved its slow pace forward.

Finally the babble—as it reached Thomas and his men—broke
into the pieces of excited conversation.

"Demons upon us!"

"We are fated to doom!"

"Pray the Lord takes mercy upon us!"

Then, like the eye of an ominous storm, the voices immediately in front died. That sudden calmness chilled Thomas more than the most agitated words which had reached his ears.

Within sixty more paces, he understood the horrified silence.

Thomas felt rooted at the sight, and only the pressure of movement behind him kept him in motion.

To the side of the steady motion of the column stood a small clearing. Facing the column, as if ready to charge, and stuck solidly on iron bars imbedded into the ground, were the massive heads of two white bulls.

Blood—in dried rivulets on the iron bars—had pooled beneath the heads. Swarmed flies gorged on the thick brown-red liquid, beneath the line of vision of the open and sightless eyes of each head.

The remains of a huge fire scarred the grass between the heads. Little remained of its fuel, but charred hooves carefully arranged outward in a circle left little doubt that the bodies of the animals had been burned.

Thomas looked upward. Again a chill of the unnatural nearly froze his steps.

At first, it appeared as heavy ribbons hanging from the branches of a nearby tree. Then, as Thomas focused closer, he fought the urge to retch. Draped as countlessly as leaves, short pieces of the entrails of the bulls swayed lightly in the wind.

Carved clearly into the trunk of the tree was the strange symbol of conspiracy, the one which matched the ring of the Earl of York.

Thomas closed his eyes in cold fear. Words spat with hatred by Geoffrey echoed through his head.

"Already the forces of darkness gather to reconquer Magnus."

He shivered again beneath the hot blue sky.

8

"This had better be good," growled Frederick. His jowls wobbled with each word. "Anything to make these peasants forget this morning's unholy remains of two white bulls."

White bulls—rare and valuable beyond compare—suggested a special power that appealed to even the least superstitious peasants. What demons might be invoked with such a carefully arranged slaughter of the animals?

It was a question asked again and again throughout the morning. Now, with the army at midday rest, nothing else would be discussed.

Thomas felt the pressure. He faced the barons and earls around him. "If each of you would, please summon your strongest and best—"

"Swordsmen?" Frederick sneered. "I'll offer to fight you myself."

"Yeomen," Thomas stated.

"Bah. An archery contest. Where's the blood in that?"

"Precisely," Thomas said. He wondered briefly how the fat

man had ever become an earl. Even a child—if they wished to accuse him of that—would have a better understanding of war. "How does it serve our purpose to draw blood among ourselves when the enemy waits to do the same?"

The reply drew scattered laughs. Someone clapped Thomas on the back. "Well spoken, puppy!"

The fat man would not be deterred. "What might a few arrows prove? Everyone knows battles are won in the glory of the charge. In the nobility of holding the front line against a countercharge. Man against man. Beast against beast. Bravery against bravery until the enemy flees."

Thomas noticed stirrings of agreement from the other earls and barons. He *did* feel like a puppy among starving dogs. Yet he welcomed the chance to argue a method of warfare which had well served generals two oceans away nearly 2,000 years earlier.

"Man against man? Beast against beast?" Thomas countered as he thought of the books of knowledge which had won him Magnus. "Lives do not matter?"

"*We* command from safety," Frederick said with smugness. "Our lives matter and are well protected. It has always been done in this manner."

Thomas drew a breath. Was it his imagination, or was the Earl of York—still silent—enjoying this argument? It was a thought which gave him new determination.

"There are better methods," Thomas said quickly. He removed all emotion from his voice and the flattening of his words drew total attention.

"The bulk of this army—and any other—consists of poorly trained farmers and villagers. None with armor. How they must fear the battle."

"The fear makes them fight harder!" Frederick snorted.

"Knowing they are to be sacrificed like sheep?"

"I repeat," Frederick said. "It has always been done in this manner."

"Listen," Thomas said, now with urgency. He knew as he spoke that some of the earls were considering his words carefully. *If he could present his argument clearly . . .*

"If these men knew you sought to win battles and preserve their lives, loyalty and love would make them far better soldiers than fear of death."

"But—"

Thomas would breach no interruption. "Furthermore, man against man, beast against beast dictates that the largest and strongest army will win."

"Of course. Any simpleton knows that," Frederick said, voice laced with scorn.

"And should we find ourselves the lesser army of the two?"

Silence.

Thomas quoted from a passage of one of his secret books. "The art of using troops is this. When ten to the enemy's one, surround him; when five times his strength, attack him; if double his strength, divide him; if equally matched, you may engage him; if weaker in numbers, be capable of withdrawing; and if in all respects unequal, be capable of eluding him."

The Earl of York smiled openly at the slack-jawed mouths in response to the quote.

Thomas did not notice. Instead, he searched his memory for the final quote. "All war is deception. What is of supreme importance in war is to attack the enemy's strategy. *And the supreme art of war is to subdue the enemy without fighting.*"

More silence.

The fat one recovered first. "Bah. Words. Simply words. What have they to do with an archery contest?"

"Let me demonstrate," Thomas said with much more confidence than he felt. "Gather, each one of you, your best archer."

The opposing fourteen bowmen lined up first. Each had been chosen for height and strength. Longer arms drew a bow string back farther, which meant more distance. Stronger arms were steadier, which meant better accuracy.

Seven targets were set two hundred yards away. People packed both sides of the field, so that the space to the targets appeared as a wide alley of untrampled grass.

Without fanfare, the first seven of the selected archers fired. Five of the seven arrows pierced completely the leather shields set up as targets. One arrow hit the target, but bounced off—a good enough feat to be acknowledged with brief applause. The other arrow flew barely wide, and quivered to a rest in the ground behind the targets.

The results of such fine archery drew gasps, even from a crowd experienced in warfare.

The next seven archers accomplished almost the same. Five more arrows pierced the targets. The other two flew high and beyond. More gasps.

Then Thomas and his men stepped to the firing line.

In direct contrast, Thomas had chosen small men with shorter arms. That the contrast was obvious became apparent by murmurs swelling from the crowd.

Thomas stood at the line with his fourteen men. He spoke in low tones heard only by them. "You have practiced much. Yet I would prefer that we attempt nothing which alarms you."

He paused and studied them. Each returned his look with a smile.

Smiles? "You enjoy this?" Thomas asked.

They nodded. "We know these weapons well," one said. "Such a demonstration will set men on their ears."

Thomas grinned in relief. "Then I propose this. We will request that the targets be moved back until the first of you says no farther. Thus, none of you will fear the range."

More smiles and nods. Thomas then turned and shouted down the field. "More distance!"

He noted with satisfaction the renewed murmuring from the crowd. The men at the targets stopped ten steps back and began to position them in place.

"Farther!" Thomas commanded.

Louder murmurs. The best archers in an army of thousands had already shot at maximum range!

"Farther!" Thomas shouted when the men with targets paused. Five steps, ten steps, twenty steps. Finally, one of the archers whispered the range was enough. By then, the targets were nearly a quarter of the distance farther than they had been set originally.

The crowd knew such range was impossible. Expectant silence replaced disbelieving murmurs.

Thomas made no person wait. He dropped his hand, and within seconds a flurry of arrows hissed toward the leather shields.

Few spectators were able to turn their heads quickly enough to follow the arrows.

Twelve arrows thudded solidly home. One arrow drove through the shield completely, spraying stripped feathers in all directions. The final two arrows overshot the targets and landed twenty yards farther down.

Thomas wanted to jump with joy and amazement, as were many in the crowd.

Instead, he turned calmly to his archers and raised his voice to be heard. He smiled. "Survey the crowd and remember this for your grandchildren. It's not often in a lifetime so few are able to set so many on their ears."

9

The northward march began again. Memory of the slaughter of two white bulls faded quickly, it seemed, and all tongues spoke only of the archery contest.

Thomas and his men had little time to enjoy their sudden fame, however. Barely an hour later, the column of people slowed, then stopped.

Low grumbling rose. Some strained to see ahead, hoping to find reason for the delay. Others—older and wiser—flopped themselves into the shade beneath trees and sought sleep.

Thomas, on horseback, near his men, saw the runner approaching from a long distance ahead. As he neared, Thomas saw the man's eyes rolling white with exhaustion.

"Sire!" he stumbled and panted. "The Earl of York wishes you to join him at the front!"

"Do you need to reach more commanders down the line?" Thomas asked.

The man heaved for breath, and could only nod.

Thomas nodded at a boy beside him. "Take this man's message," he instructed. "Please relay it to the others and give him rest."

With that, Thomas wheeled his horse forward, and cantered alongside the column. Small spurts of dust kicked from the horse's hooves; the sheer number of people, horses, and mules passing through the moors had already packed and worn the grass to its roots.

Thomas spotted the Earl of York's banners at the front of the army column quickly enough. About half of the other earls were gathered around. Their horses stood nearby, heads bent to graze on the grass yet untrampled by the army.

Thomas swung down from the horse, and strode to join them. For the second time that day, a chill prickled his scalp.

Three men stood in front of the Earl of York and the others. They only wore torn and filthy pants. No shoes, no shirt or cloak. Each of the three were gray-white with fear, and unable to stand without help.

The chill that shook Thomas, however, did not result from their obvious fear or weakness. Instead, he could not take his eyes from the circular welts centered on the flesh of their chests.

"They've been branded!" Thomas blurted.

"Aye, Thomas. Our scouts found them bound to these trees." The Earl of York nodded in the direction of nearby oaks.

Thomas stared with horror at the three men. The brand marks nearly spanned the width of each chest. The burned flesh stood raised with an angry, dark puffiness.

Thomas sucked in a breath.

Each brand showed the strange symbol.

"Who . . . who . . ."

"Who did this, you wish to ask," the Earl of York finished for Thomas.

Thomas nodded. He fought the urge to glance at the earl's hand to confirm what he didn't want to believe. *The symbol* which matched the earl's ring. The symbol carved into the tree near the two white bulls' heads. The symbol of conspiracy.

"It is impossible to tell who did this to these men," the Earl of York answered his own question. "Impossible to understand why they have been left for us to find."

"Impossible?" Thomas could barely concentrate. *Already the forces of darkness gather . . .*

"Yes. Impossible. Their tongues have been removed." The earl shook his head sadly. "Poor men. And of course they cannot write. We shall feed and rest them, and let them return to their homes."

Could the Earl of York be this fine an actor to stand in front of these tortured men and pretend he had no part of the symbol? Or was his ring simply a bizarre coincidence?

The earl wiped his face clean of sweat.

His ring. Gone.

A wide band of white marked where the earl had worn it.

Thomas shook off the feeling of being utterly alone.

Surprisingly, Frederick—Frederick the Fat as Thomas silently called him—proved to be a gracious loser at the council of war held in the evening.

"This puppy has the teeth of a dragon," he toasted in the direction of Thomas.

"Hear, hear," the others responded.

Again, the light of countless campfires spread like flashing diamonds through the valley. Still four days away from the lowland plains and any chance of battle, the army had not dug in behind palisades, and tents were still pitched far enough apart so that neighbors did not have to stumble over neighbors as they searched for firewood or water.

Thomas accepted the compliment with equal graciousness. "As you rightly guessed," he said to Frederick, "the power lies within the bows, not the archers."

"Still," Frederick countered, "and I can say it because he is not here with us, the Earl of York has again proven his wisdom. I erred to judge you on size or age."

Thomas shrugged. Not necessarily from modesty, but rather because the idea for the ingenious modification of the bows had simply been taken straight from one of his secret books.

As a result, running the length of the inside of each bow, Thomas had added a strip of wide thin bronze, giving more strength than the firmest wood. His biggest difficulty had been finding a drawstring which would not snap under the strain of such a powerful bow.

"But such archery will prove little in this battle." The earl sitting beside Frederick interrupted Thomas in his thoughts. "You have only twenty bows with such a capacity for distance."

Thomas laughed. "Do the Scots know that? They will only understand arrows suddenly reaching them from an unheard of distance long beyond their own range. Even if they knew our shortage of these bows, each man on the opposing line still realizes it only takes one arrow to pierce his heart. Surely there is benefit in that."

"Yes." Another earl sipped his broth, then continued in support of Thomas. "The man we have dubbed Sir Puppy—"

General laughter. Thomas knew immediately it was a name of affection and honor. He smiled in return.

". . . named Sir Puppy earlier spoke of battle tactics which interest me keenly. I see clearly that even a few of these bows can affect warfare."

The Earl of York strode to the campfire as that statement finished. All rose in respect.

"You do well, Sir Steven, to make mention of the tactics of

war," the Earl of York said grimly in response. "I have just received word from our scouts. It isn't enough to be plagued by the evils of slain white bulls and tongueless men. The Scots' army numbers over 4,000 strong."

Silence deepened as each man realized the implications of that news. They numbered barely 3,000. *Man against man. Beast against beast. And outnumbered by a thousand. They would be fortunate to survive.*

The Earl of York, as was his due, spoke first to break the silence. "Perhaps our boy warrior, Thomas of Magnus, has a suggestion."

The implied honor nearly staggered Thomas. To receive a request for council among these men . . . yet was the Earl of York a friend or foe? And if a foe, why the honor?

"Thank you, sire," Thomas replied, more to gain time and calmness than from gratitude. *To throw away this chance . . .*

Thomas thought hard. *These men understand force and force alone. This much I have learned.*

Another thought flashed through his mind, a story of war told him by his long dead friend and nurse, a story from one of the books of ancient knowledge.

He hid a grin in the darkness. Each man at the campfire waited in silence, each pair of eyes studied him.

Finally, Thomas spoke.

"We can defeat the Scots," he said. "First, we must convince them we are cowards."

1 0

Sleep came upon Thomas quickly that night.

He dreamed of Sarah, who had taught him through his childhood, had given him love while he suffered as an orphan, and had prepared him for a lordship before she died of the pox.

He dreamed of Katherine, dirty bandages around the horribly scarred flesh of her face, and how she, at the end, had made it possible for him to conquer Magnus.

It was no surprise then that Thomas imagined he was not alone in the tent.

And slowly, he woke to perfume and the softness of hair falling across his face.

He drew breath to challenge the intruder, but a light finger across his lips, and a gentle shushing stopped him from speaking.

"Dress quickly, Thomas. Follow without protest," the voice then whispered.

Thomas saw only the darkness of silhouette in the dimness of the tent.

"Fear not," the voice continued. "An old man wishes to see you. He asks if you remember the gallows."

Old man! Gallows! In a rush of memory as bright as daylight, Thomas felt himself at the gallows. The knight who might win for him Magnus about to be hanged, and Thomas in front, there to attempt a rescue through disguise and trickery. Then the arrival of an old man, one who knew it was Thomas behind the disguise and knew of his quest, one who had commanded the sun into darkness, one who had never appeared again.

"As you wish," Thomas whispered in return with as much dignity as he could muster despite the sudden trembling in his stomach. No mystery—not even the evil terror of the strange symbol—was more important to him than discovering the old man's identity.

The silhouette backed away slowly, beckoning Thomas with a single crooked finger. He rose quickly, wrapped his cloak around him, and shuffled into his shoes.

How had she avoided the sentries outside his tent?

Thomas pushed aside the flap of the tent and followed. Her perfume hung in the heavy night air.

Moonlight showed that both sentries sat crookedly against the base of a nearby tree. *Asleep!* It was within his rights as lord to have them executed.

"Forgive them," the voice whispered as if reading his mind. "Their suppers contained potions of drowsiness."

He strained to see the face of the silhouette in the light of the large pale moon. In response, she pulled the flaps of her hood across her face. All he saw was a tall and slender figure, leading him slowly along a trail which avoided all tents and campsites.

Ghost-white snakes of mist hung heavy among the solitary trees of the moor valley.

It felt too much like a dream to Thomas. Still, he did not fear to follow. Only one person had knowledge of what had transpired in front of the gallows—the old man himself. Only he, then, could have sent the silhouette to his tent.

At the farthest edge of the camp she stopped to turn and wait. When Thomas arrived, she took his right hand and clasped it with both hands.

"Who are you?" Thomas asked. "Show me your face."

"Hush, Thomas," she whispered.

"You know my name. You know my face. Yet you hide from me."

"Hush," she repeated.

"No," he said with determination. "Not a step farther will I take. The old man wishes to see me badly enough to drug my sentries. He will be angry if you do not succeed in your mission."

She did not answer. Instead, she lifted her hand slowly, pulled the hood from her face, and shook her hair loose to her shoulders.

Nothing in his life had prepared him for that moment.

The sudden ache of joy to see her face hit him like a blow. For a timeless moment, it took from him all breath.

It was not her beauty which brought him that joy, even though the curved shadows of her face would be forever seared in his mind. No. Thomas knew he had learned not to trust appearances, that beauty indeed consisted of heart joining heart, not eyes to eyes. Isabelle, now in the dungeon, had used her exquisite features to deceive, while gentle Katherine—horribly burned and masked by bandages—had proven the true worth of friendship.

Thomas struggled for composure. *What then drew him? Why did it seem as if he had been long pledged for this very moment?*

She stared back, as if knowing completely how he felt, yet fearless of the voltage between them. Then she smiled, and pulled the hood across her face once again.

"Was it enough?"

Thomas bit his lip to keep inside a cry of emotion he could barely comprehend. Isabelle's betrayal of Magnus now seemed a childish pain. He drew dignity around him like a shield.

"The old man wishes to see me," he finally answered in stiff tones to her slightly amused voice.

She led him by the hand and picked faultless footsteps through ground soon darkened from the moon by the trees along the stream of the valley.

They walked—it could have only been a heartbeat, he felt so distant from the movement of time—until reaching a hill which rose steeply into the black of the night.

An owl called.

She turned to the sound, and walked directly into the side of the hill. As if parting the solid rock by magic, she slipped sideways into an invisible cleft between monstrous boulders. Thomas followed.

They stood completely surrounded by granite walls of a cave long hollowed smooth by eons of rain water. The air seemed to press down upon him, and away from the light of the moon, Thomas saw only velvet black.

He heard the returning call of an owl leave her lips, and before he could react to the noise, there was a small spark. His eyes adjusted to see an old man holding the small light of a torch which grew as the pitch caught fire.

1 1

Light gradually licked upward around them to reveal a bent old man, wrapped in a shawl. Beyond deep wrinkles, Thomas could distinguish no features—the shadows leapt and danced eerie circles from beneath his chin.

"Greetings, Thomas of Magnus." The voice was a whisper.

"Who are you?"

"Such impatience. One who is Lord of Magnus would do well to temper his words among strangers."

"I cannot apologize," Thomas said. "Each day I am haunted by memory of you. Impossible that you should know my quest at the hanging. Impossible that the sun should fail that morning at your command."

The old man shrugged and continued in the same strained whisper. "Impossible is often merely a perception. Surely by now you have been able to ascertain the darkness was no sorcery, but merely a trick of astronomy as the moon moves past the sun. Your books would inform a careful reader that such eclipses may be predicted."

"You know of my books! How?"

The old man ignored the urgency in Thomas' words. "My message is the same as before. You must bring the winds of light into this age, and resist the forces of darkness poised to take from you the kingdom of Magnus. Yet what assistance I may offer is little—the decisions to be made are yours."

Thomas clenched his fists and exhaled a frustrated blast of air. "You talk in circles. Tell me who you are. Tell me clearly what you want of me. And tell me the secret of Magnus."

Again, Thomas' words were ignored.

"Druids, Thomas. Beware those barbarians from the isle. They will attempt to conquer you through force. Or bribery."

"If I do not go insane because of your games," Thomas said through gritted teeth, "it will be a miracle. Tell me how you knew of my quest that day at the hanging. Tell me how you know of the books. Tell me how you know of the barbarians."

"To tell you is to risk all."

Thomas pounded his thigh in anger. *I do not even know what is at risk!* You set upon me a task unexplained, and give me no reason to fulfill it! I must have knowledge!"

Even in his frustration, Thomas sensed the old man's sadness.

"The knowledge you already have is worth the world, Thomas. That is all I can say."

"No," Thomas pleaded. *The old man must know more.* "Who belongs to the strange symbol of conspiracy? Is the Earl of York friend or enemy?"

The old man shook his head. "Very soon you will be offered a prize which seems far greater than the kingdom of Magnus."

The torch flared once before dying, and Thomas read deep concern in the old man's eyes. From the sudden darkness came his final whispered words. "It is worth your soul to refuse."

1 2

In daylight, Thomas took advantage of the frenzied preparations to break camp. He slipped away and scrambled along the valley stream, searching for the cleft in the rock that had led him to the midnight meeting.

He had no success. The daylight disoriented him—nothing seemed familiar. He walked back, wondering if the night before had been a dream, and hoping it had not. He only had to close his eyes to remember the shadows of her face, and her gently whispered farewell.

Thomas was given little time to ponder the event. Immediately upon his return, a servant led to him his horse. Thomas mounted, and trotted alongside his army as the massed march moved forward, creaky and bulky, but now with a sense of urgency. The enemy waited three days ahead.

Repeatedly during the day, the Earl of York wheeled his horse beside Thomas and relayed new battle information, or confirmed old. It was a clear sign to the other earls that Thomas was fully part of the council of war. Yet Thomas wondered. Did the Earl of York have other reasons for pretending friendliness?

Thomas also noticed how little was the laughter and singing in the marching column. No one had forgotten the grisly sights of the previous day.

Druids, the old man had said. *Beware those barbarians from the isle.*

Were they the ones of the strange symbol and the terrifying acts of brutality?

As Thomas swayed to the gentle walk of his horse, he decided there was a way to find out, even if the old man of mystery never appeared again.

First, however, there was the formal council of war as camp was made that evening.

The Earl of York wasted no time once all were gathered. "After tonight, there are only two nights before battle. Each of you have reduced by a third the fires in your camps?" he asked.

In turn, each lesser earl nodded, including Thomas.

"Good, good," the Earl of York said. "Already their spies are in the hills. Observing. Waiting."

"You know this to be true?" Frederick asked with slight surprise.

The Earl of York snorted. "Our own spies have been reporting for days now. Only a fool would expect the enemy not to do the same."

"Their fires," Thomas said. "What word?"

"The valleys they choose for camp are filled as if by daylight."

Silence as each contemplated the odds of death against such an army.

The Earl of York did not permit the mood to lengthen. He continued his questions in the tone which made them sound like orders. "All of you have brave volunteers ready to desert our army?"

Each, again, nodded.

"Tomorrow, then," the Earl of York said, "is the day. Let half of them melt away into the forest. The rest on the following day."

He paused. "Slumber in peace, gentlemen. Dream only of victory."

While all began to leave, the earl moved forward and discreetly tugged on Thomas' sleeve.

"If this battle plan works, friend, your reward will be countless. If not . . ." The earl smiled the smile of a fighter who has won and lost many times. "It shall be man against man, beast against beast. What say you to that?"

"Then I shall fight bravely, m'lord."

"No, Thomas. What say you to a reward? Let us prepare ourselves for the best. Ask now. What is your wish?"

Thomas thought of the ring. The symbol. And Druids.

Was the Earl of York part of the conspiracy to reconquer Magnus? If so, would he still honor a promise made?

"Reward?" Thomas repeated quietly. "I would wish after the battle that you simply spoke truth to a simple question."

The earl's jaw dropped. He recovered quickly. "You have my word of honor." Then he dryly added, "My friend, in fairy tales most men ask for the daughter's hand."

Thomas snorted at that unexpected reply. During that moment, he felt at ease with the older man. "I would fear, m'lord, that the daughter might resemble too closely her father."

The earl slapped his belly and roared laughter. "Thomas! You are a man among men. I see a destiny for the likes of you."

Surely this man could not be one of them.

She was the oldest woman he could find during a hurried search of the other campsites as the last of dusk quickly settled.

Even in the lowered light, Thomas saw the grease that caked deep wrinkles on her hands and fingers. A cook, no doubt. Part of the army which serves an army.

She sat, leaning her back against a stone which jutted from the flattened grass. Her shabby gray cloak did not have a hood and her hair had thinned enough so that her scalp stretched shiny and tight in the firelight, an ugly contrast to the skin which hung in wattles from her cheeks and jaw.

"Ho! Ho!" she cackled as Thomas stopped in front of her. "Have all the young women spurned your company? Tsk. Tsk. And such a handsome devil you are." She took a gulp from a leather bag. "Come closer, dearie. Share my wine!"

Thomas moved closer, but shook his head no. She smelled of many days squatting in front of a cookfire, and of many weeks unbathed.

She snatched the wine back and gulped again. Then cocked her head. "You'd be Thomas of Magnus. The boy warrior. I remember from the archery contest." Another gulp. "I'll not rise to bow. At my age, there is little to fear. Not even the displeasure of an earl or lord." She finished with a coughing wheeze.

The old, instinct told Thomas, *will know the tales you need, the tales you did not hear the night before.*

So he asked. "Druids. Would you fear Druids?"

The old crone clutched her wine bag, then took a slower swallow and gazed thoughtfully at Thomas. From deep within her face, black eyes glittered traces of the nearby campfire.

"Druids?" she hissed. "That is a name to be spoken only with great care. Where would someone so young get a name so ancient and so forgotten?"

"The burnings of two white bulls," Thomas guessed. He was still working on instinct, and the old man in the cave had not connected Druids with those sights. "Three men now mute."

"Nay, lad. A host of others in this army have seen the same. Not once have I heard the name of those evil sorcerers cross any lips."

Evil sorcerers!

"So," she continued. "It is not from their rituals you offer that name, although from the talk I hear none have guessed so true. Confess, boy. How is it you know what none others perceive?"

He was right. Druids were behind the symbol. That meant then, Druids were behind the conspiracy to take Magnus. What might this old, old woman know of their tales . . .

Thomas did not flinch at her stare. *Keep her speaking,* he commanded himself. He tried to bluff. "Perhaps one merely has knowledge of their usual activities."

The crone revealed her gums in a wide smile. "But of course, you're from Magnus."

Thomas froze and every nerve ending tingled. *Magnus. Druids. As if it were natural that there was a connection between the two.*

"What," he asked through a tightened jaw, "would such imply?"

"Hah! You do know less than you pretend!" The crone patted the ground beside her. "Come. Sit. Listen to what my own grandmother once told me."

Thomas moved beside her. A bony hand clutched his knee.

"There have been over a hundred winters since she was a young girl," the old crone said of her grandmother. "When she told me these tales, she had become as old then as I am now. Generations have passed and died since her youth then and my old age now. In that time, common knowledge of those ancient sorcerers has disappeared. Even in my grandmother's youth, she told me, Druids were rarely spoken of. And now . . ."

The crone shrugged. "Yet *you* come now with questions." The bony hand squeezed and she asked abruptly, "Do you seek their black magic?"

"It is the farthest thing from my desires."

"I hear truth in your words, boy. Let me then continue."

Thomas waited. So close to answers, it did not matter how

badly she smelled. His heart thudded, and for a moment, he wondered if she heard.

Then she began again. Her breath washed over Thomas, hot and oddly sweet from wine. " 'Druid' means Finder of the Oak Tree. It is where they gather, deep in the forests to begin their rituals. I was told that their circle of high priest and sorcerers began long ago in the mists of time, on the isle of the Celts. They study philosophy, astronomy, and the lore of the gods."

Astronomy! The old man in the cave had known enough astronomy to predict the eclipse of the sun!

Thomas stood and paced, then realized her voice had stopped. "I'm sorry," he said. "Please, please continue."

"They also offer human sacrifices for the sick or for those in danger of death in battle." The crone crossed herself and swallowed more wine in the same motion. "I remember the fear in my grandmother's eyes as she told me. And the legends still persist. Whispers among the very old. It is said that when the Romans overran our island—before the time of the Saxons and before the time of the Viking raiders—they forced the Druids to accept Christianity. But that was merely appearance. Through the hundreds of years, the circle of high priests held on to their knowledge of the ways of evil. Once openly powerful, now they remain hidden."

Thomas could not contain himself longer. "Magnus!" he said. "You spoke of Magnus."

Her hand clutched his knee one final time, then relaxed. From her came a soft laugh. "Bring me a feast tomorrow. Rich meat. Cheese. Buttered bread. And much wine. That is my price for the telling of ancient tales."

After a cackle of glee, she dropped her head to her chest, and soon began to snore.

1 3

Thomas washed back the last of his mutton stew with ale as he finished supper on the second to last night before the lowland plains. Tomorrow, the army would travel until late afternoon, camp, and prepare for battle the following day.

Much was on his mind. The wonderful ache which he could not ignore because of someone who had led him to the old man. The mystery of the old man himself. What he might learn from the old woman. And how the battle against the Scots would end.

His men respected his quiet mood and gave him peace. They stood or sat in small groups around the fire, trading oft-repeated stories in softer voices than the night before. The older men especially—those who had seen friends die in other battles—said little this close to the lowland plains north of the moors.

"Your provisions, sir," a dirt-streaked servant girl said with her head down.

"Thank you," Thomas said. He accepted the cloth bag and noted with satisfaction its heavy weight. The old crone would be well paid for her tales.

He stood briskly and walked through the graying light to seek her.

Thomas smiled grimly to see that there were fewer campfires again than the night before. The Earl of York's orders had been obeyed with precision.

The area of the camp had been reduced too, and it took little time for Thomas to recognize the banners of the earl whose army held a cackling, dirty crone with tales that stretched back six generations.

Thomas strode around the fires once, then twice. No one interfered; his colors clearly marked him as an earl, and avoiding the eye of those in power usually resulted in less work.

Finally, he was forced to attract the attention of a man carrying buckets of water hanging from each end of a pole balanced across his shoulders.

"Tell me, please," Thomas said. "Where rests the old cook?"

"A day's travel behind us, m'lord." The man grimaced. "Just more duty for some of us now."

Thomas squinted to read the man's face. "She deserted camp?"

"No, m'lord. She was found dead this morning." The man crossed himself quickly. "Rest her soul."

"That cannot be!"

The man shrugged, a motion that shook both buckets of water. "Too much wine and too much age. It came as no surprise."

Thomas clamped his mouth shut, then nodded his thanks.

What had the crone said? *Druids. That is a name to be spoken only with great care.*

Surely her death was coincidence. Too much wine and too much age and the rigors of daily march. Of course.

Still, Thomas glanced around him often at the deepening shadows as he hurried to his tent and the welcome sentries.

14

Late afternoon the next day, Thomas joined the Earl of York at the head of the army column.

From the backs of their horses they overlooked yet another moor valley.

"Thus far, our calculations have served us well," the Earl of York said. "Scouts report the Scottish army is barely a half day away. And beyond here, the moors end at the plains."

Thomas nodded and shaded his eyes with one hand. Sunlight poured over the western hills. "This *does* appear to be the perfect place to ambush an army," Thomas said. "High sloping hills—impossible to climb under enemy fire. Narrow entrances at both ends—easy to guard against escape. Your scouts excelled in their choice."

Thomas nodded again, and for a moment, both enjoyed the breeze sweeping toward them from the mouth of the valley.

"Well, then. We have made our choice." The Earl of York sighed. "Any army trapped within it is sure to be slaughtered."

He turned and called to the men behind him.

"Send a runner back with directions. We shall camp ahead."
He lifted a hand to point. "There. In the center of the valley."

Then quietly, he spoke again to Thomas. "Let us pray the
valley does not earn a new name in our honor," the Earl of York
said with a shudder. "The valley of death."

Thomas shuddered with him. But for a different reason. Even
after several days of travel, it still seemed too bright, the pale
band of skin on the earl's finger where he had so recently worn
a ring.

1 5

A deep drum roll of thousands of hooves shook the earth and dawn broke pale blue with the thunder of impending war.

The screams of trumpets ordered the direction of the men and beasts which poured into both ends of the valley. High banners proudly led column after column after column of foot soldiers four abreast, every eye intent on the helpless encampment of tents and dying fires in the center of the valley.

It immediately became obvious that much thought had gone into the lightning-quick maneuver. Amid shouting and clamor, men and horses moved into rows which were hundreds wide.

Like a giant pincer, the great army closed in on the camp.

When it finished—barely twenty minutes later—the pincer consisted of a deep front row of pikesmen. Behind them, hundreds of archers. Behind the archers, knights on horses.

At first light with stunning swiftness, it was a surprise attack well designed to catch the enemy heavy with sleep.

Finally, a great banner rose upward on a long pole. Every man in the Scottish army became silent.

An entire valley filled with men intent on death, yet in the still air of early morning, the only sound was the occasional stamping of an impatient horse. It made for an eeriness that sent shivers along the backs of even the most experienced Scot warriors.

Then a strong voice broke that silence. "Surrender in the name of Robert Bruce, king of the Scots!"

The tents of the trapped army hung limp under the weight of dew. Not one flap stirred in response. Smoke wafted from fires almost dead. A dog scurried from one garbage pit to another.

"Discuss surrender!" the voice continued. "Or die in the tents that hide you!"

Moments passed. Many of the warriors found themselves holding their breaths. Fighting might be noble and glorious, but to win without risking death was infinitely better.

"The third blast of the trumpet will signal our charge. Unless you surrender before then, all hell will be loosed upon you!"

The trumpet blew once.

Then twice.

And at the edge of the camp, a tent flap opened and a figure stepped outside, to begin striding toward the huge army. From a hundred yards away, the figure appeared to be a slender man, unencumbered with armor or weapons. He walked without apparent fear to the voice which had summoned him.

Thomas could barely comprehend the sight as he walked. Filling the horizon in all directions were men and lances and armor and horses and banners and swords and shields and pikes.

Directly ahead, the men of the opposing council of war. Among them, the man who had demanded surrender with that strong clear voice.

Thomas tried driving his fear away, but could not. *Was this his day to die?*

He could guess at the sight he presented to the men on horseback watching his approach. He had not worn the cloak bearing the colors of Magnus. Instead, he had dressed as poorly as a stable boy. Better for the enemy to think him a lowly messenger. Especially for what needed to be done.

There were roughly a dozen gathered. They moved their horses ahead of their army, to be recognized as the men of power. Each horse was covered in colored blankets. Each man in light armor. They were not heavily protected fighters; they were leaders.

Thomas forced himself ahead, step by step.

The spokesman identified himself immediately. He had a bristling red beard and eyes of fire to match. He stared at Thomas with the fierceness of a hawk, and his rising anger became obvious.

"The Earl of York hides in his tent like a woman and sends to us a boy?"

"I am Thomas. Of Magnus. I bring a message from the Earl of York."

The quiet politeness seemed to check the Scot's rage. He blinked once, then said, "I am Kenneth of Carlisle."

Thomas was close enough now that he had to crane his head upward to speak to the one with the red beard.

Sunlight glinted from heavy battle axes.

"Kenneth of Carlisle," Thomas said with the same dignity, "the Earl of York is not among the tents."

This time, the bearded earl spoke almost with sadness. "I am sorry to hear he is a coward."

"He is not, m'lord. May we speak in private?"

"There is nothing to discuss," Kenneth said. "Accept our terms of surrender. Or the entire camp is doomed."

"Sir," Thomas persisted, hands wide and palms upward. "As you can see, I bear no arms. I can do you no harm."

Hesitation. Then a glint of curiosity from those fierce eyes.

"Hold all the men," Kenneth of Carlisle commanded, then dismounted from his horse. Despite the covering of light armor, he swung down with grace.

Thomas stepped back several paces to allow them privacy.

Kenneth of Carlisle advanced and towered above Thomas. "What is it you can possibly plead which needs such quiet discussion?"

"I mean no disrespect, m'lord," Thomas said in low tones, "but the surrender which needs discussing is yours."

16

Five heartbeats of silence.

The huge man slowly lifted his right hand as if to strike Thomas, then lowered it.

"I understand." Yellow teeth gleamed from his beard as he snorted disdain. "You attempt to slay me with laughter."

"No," Thomas answered. "Too many lives are at stake."

Suddenly Kenneth of Carlisle clapped his hands down on Thomas' shoulders and shook him fiercely. "Then play no games!" he shouted.

That surge of temper ended as quickly as it had arrived, and the shaking stopped.

Thomas took a breath. "This is no game." He looked past Kenneth of Carlisle at the others nearby on their horses. They stared back with puzzled frowns.

"I am here to present you with a decision," Thomas continued again to the bearded man. "One you must consider before returning to your horse."

"I shall humor you." Kenneth of Carlisle folded his arms and waited.

"Firstly," Thomas said, "did you believe our army was at full strength?"

After a moment of consideration, the Scottish earl replied, "Certainly not. Our scouts brought daily reports of cowards fleeing your army. The deserters we captured all told us the same thing. Your entire army feared battle against us. We saw proof nightly. Your—"

"—campfires," Thomas interrupted. "Each night you saw fewer and fewer campfires. Obvious evidence of an army which shrunk each day, until last night when you may have calculated we had less than a thousand men remaining."

Kenneth of Carlisle laughed. "So few men we wondered if it would be worth our while to make this short detour for battle."

"It was the Earl of York's wish," Thomas said. He risked a quick look at the tops of the hills, then hid a smile of satisfaction.

"Eh? The Earl of York's wish?"

"Again, with much due respect, m'lord—" Thomas swept his arm wide to indicate the valley— "did it not seem too easy? A crippled army quietly camped in a valley with no means of escape?"

Momentary doubt crossed the man's face.

Thomas pressed on. "The deserters you caught had left our army by the Earl of York's commands. Each man had instructions to report great fear among the men left behind. We reduced the campfires to give the impression of mass desertion. While our fires are few, our men remain many."

The news startled Kenneth of Carlisle enough for him to flinch.

"Furthermore," Thomas said, "none of those men are here in the valley. Each tent is empty. In the dark of night, all crept away."

Five more heartbeats of silence.

"Impossible," blurted Kenneth of Carlisle. But the white which replaced the red of flushed skin above his beard showed that the man suddenly considered it very possible, and did not like the implications.

Thomas kept his voice calm. "By now"—Thomas resisted the urge to look and reconfirm what he already knew—"those men have reached their new positions. They block the exits at both ends of this valley and line the tops of the surrounding hills."

"Impossible." This time, his tone of voice was weaker.

"Impossible, m'lord? Survey the hills."

This was the most important moment of the battle. *Would the huge man be stunned at their desperate bluff?*

What he and Thomas saw from the valley floor seemed awesome. Stretched across the entire line of the tops of the hills on each side of the valley men were stepping into sight in full battle gear. From the viewpoint below, those men were simply dark figures, made small by distance. But the line was solid in both directions and advancing downward slowly.

The Earl of York had timed it perfectly.

"Impossible," Kenneth of Carlisle said for the third time. There was, however, no doubt in his voice.

Murmuring rose from around them as others noticed the movement. Soon word had spread throughout the entire army. Men started shifting nervously.

"The Earl of York's army will not advance farther," Thomas promised. "Not unless they have reason."

Thomas also knew if the Earl of York's army moved any closer, the thinness of the advancing line would soon become obvious. The row was only two warriors deep—as many as possible had been sent away from the line to block the escapes at both ends of the valley.

"We shall give them reason," Kenneth of Carlisle swore intensely as he drew his sword. "Many will die today!"

"And many more of yours, m'lord."

Kenneth of Carlisle glared and with both hands buried half the blade of the sword into the ground in front of Thomas.

Thomas waited until the sword stopped quivering. "M'lord," he said, hoping the rush of his own fear would not be heard in his voice. "I requested a discussion in privacy so that you and I could reconsider any such words spoken harshly in the heat of anger."

Kenneth of Carlisle glared harder, but made no further moves.

"Consider this," Thomas said. "The entrances to the valley are so narrow that to reach one of our men, twenty of yours must fall. Neither is it possible for your men to fight upward against the slope of these hills. Again, you would lose twenty to the Earl of York's one."

"Warfare here in the center of the valley will be more even," Kenneth of Carlisle stated flatly. "That will decide the battle."

Thomas shook his head. "The Earl of York has no intention of bringing the battle to you."

Thomas remembered a quote from one of his secret books, the one which had given him the idea for this battle plan. *The skilled commander takes up a position from which he cannot be defeated . . . thus a victorious army wins its victories before seeking battle; an army destined to defeat fights in the hope of winning.*

"The Earl of York is a coward!" Kenneth of Carlisle blustered.

"A coward to wish victory without killing his men or yours? All your supplies are behind at your main camp. His men, however, will be well fed as they wait. In two or three days, any battle will end in your slaughter."

Kenneth of Carlisle lost any semblance of controlled conversation. He roared indistinguishable sounds of rage. And when he ran out of breath, he panted a declaration of war. "We fight to the bitter end! Now!"

He turned to wave his commanders forward.

"Wait!" The cry from Thomas stopped Kenneth of Carlisle in midstride. "One final plea!"

The Scottish earl turned back, his fiery eyes flashing hatred. "A plea for your life?"

Thomas realized again how close he was to death. And again, he fought to keep his voice steady.

"No, m'lord. A plea to prevent the needless slaughter of many men." Thomas held out his hands. "If you will permit me to hold a shield."

The request was so unexpected that curiosity once more replaced fierceness. Kenneth of Carlisle called for a shield from one of his men.

Thomas grasped the bottom edge, and held it above his head, so that the top of the shield was several feet higher than his hands.

Let them see the signal, Thomas prayed. *For if a battle is declared, the Scots will too soon discover how badly we are outnumbered.*

Moments later, a half dozen men broke from the line on the hills.

"Behind you, m'lord." Thomas hoped the relief he felt was not obvious. "See the archers approach."

Kenneth of Carlisle half turned, and watched in silence.

The archers stopped three hundred yards away, too far for any features to be distinguished.

"So?" Kenneth of Carlisle said. "They hold back. More cowardice."

"No, m'lord," Thomas said, still holding the shield high. "They need come no closer."

The Scottish earl snorted. "My eyes are still sharp, puppy. They are still a sixth of a mile away."

Both watched as all six archers fitted arrows to their bows.

"Fools," Kenneth of Carlisle continued in the same derisive tone. "Fools to waste their efforts thus."

Thomas said nothing. He wanted to close his eyes, but did

not. *If but one arrow strayed* . . .

It seemed to happen in slow motion. The archers brought their bows up, drew back the arrows and let loose, all in one motion. A flash of shafts headed directly at them, then faded into nothing as the arrows became invisible against the backdrop of green hills.

Whoosh. Whoosh.

The sound arrived with the arrows and suddenly Thomas was knocked flat on his back.

For a moment, he thought he'd been struck. Yet there was no piercing pain, no blood. And he realized he'd been gripping the shield so hard from fear that the force of the arrows had bowled him over as they struck the target above his head.

Thomas quickly moved to his feet, and looked down to follow the horrified stare of Kenneth of Carlisle. Behind him on the ground lay the leather shield, penetrated completely by six arrows.

Thomas took full advantage of the awe he felt around him. "That, m'lord, is the final reason for surrender. New weaponry. From the hills, our archers will shoot at leisure, secure that your archers will never find the range to answer."

The huge Scottish earl slumped. "The terms of surrender?" he asked with resignation.

"The Earl of York simply requests you surrender your weapons. Some of your earls and dukes will be held captive for ransom, of course, but as tradition dictates, will be well treated. The foot soldiers—farmers, villagers, and peasants—will be allowed to return immediately to their families."

Kenneth of Carlisle bowed his head. "So it shall be," he said. "So it shall be."

"**Would that I had a daughter to offer,**" the Earl of York said under a wide expanse of sky broken by scattered clouds. "She and a great portion of my lands would be yours."

Thomas flushed. The earl believed it was a blush of embarrassment. But mention of marriage simply reminded Thomas of his ache to see again the midnight messenger who had led him to the old man.

"Ah, well," the Earl of York sighed. "If I cannot make you my son, at least I can content myself with your friendship."

Another flush of red. The earl believed it was a blush of modesty. Once more, Thomas knew differently. This time, he reddened to remember his suspicions.

Is this man one of the symbol? Will he betray me? Or I, him?

"Yes, yes," the Earl of York said, letting pride fill his slow words. "The legend of the boy warrior of Magnus grows. Even during the short length of our journey back from the Valley of Surrender, tales of your wisdom have been passed repeatedly from campfire to campfire."

Thomas said nothing. He did not wish credit for strategy taken from the secret knowledge which was his source of power. As well, other worries filled his heart.

Magnus lies over the next hill, he thought. *Will the Earl of York now honor his reward promised with victory?*

They rode slowly. Thomas—returning home with his small army in an orderly line behind. The earl—to retrieve his son left at Magnus as a guarantee of safety.

All the worries washed over Thomas. *Who are these Druids of the symbol? What games did the old man play—he who like the Druids knew astronomy—and from where did he gain such intimate knowledge of Thomas' life? And the castle ahead—would it provide safety against the forces of darkness which had left such terrifying sights for all to see on the march northward?*

"Your face grows heavy with dread," the Earl of York joked. "Is it because of the question which burns so plainly in your restlessness over the last few days? Rest easy, my son, I have not forgotten your strange victory request."

My son. Surely this man was not part of the darkness. . . .

Thomas steeled himself.

From the marchers behind him, voices grew higher with excitement and anticipation. This close to home, the trail winding through the moors was very familiar to the knights and foot soldiers. Within an hour, they would crest the hill above the lake which held the island castle of Magnus.

There can be no good time to ask, Thomas told himself. He went ahead, forcing his words into the afternoon breeze.

"Your ring, m'lord. The one which carries the evil symbol burned upon the chests of innocent men, the one you removed before battle. I wish to know the truth behind it."

The earl abruptly reigned his horse to a halt and stared Thomas full in the face. "Any question but that. I beg of you."

Thomas felt his heart collapse in a chill of fear and sadness. "I must, m'lord," he barely managed to whisper. "It carries a darkness which threatens me. I must know if you are friend or foe."

"Friend," the earl said with intensity. "I swear that upon my mother's grave. Can that not suffice?"

Thomas slowly shook his head.

The earl suddenly slapped his black stallion into a trot. Within seconds, Thomas rode alone.

At the entrance to the valley of Magnus, Thomas saw the Earl of York sitting on his horse beneath the shade of a tree well aside of the trail.

The Earl of York waved once, then beckoned.

Thomas slowly trotted his own horse to the tree.

The noise of travel faded behind him, and when Thomas reached the earl, he was greeted with a silence interrupted only by the buzzing of flies and a swish and slap as the other horse swung his tail to chase away those flies.

Blue of the lake surrounding Magnus broke through gaps of the low-hanging branches, and dappled shadows fell across the earl's face. It was impossible to read anything in his eyes.

"I suspect you would *not* force me to honor my vow," the earl finally said. "You have the mark of a man who lets other men live their lives as they choose."

Thomas gazed steady in return. "The man who betrays another also betrays himself. Often that is punishment enough."

The Earl of York shook his head. "From where do you get this wisdom."

"What little I have was given by a dear teacher, now dead."

More silence.

By then, almost the entire small army—in its rush to reach home—had passed along the trail. Then final puffs of dust fell to rest as the last straggler moved on, and in the quiet left behind, the earl began again.

"I have waited here in deep thought and anguish," he said. "The ring is a shameful secret passed from father to son through many generations."

He smiled weakly. "Alas, the debt I owe and a promise made justly demands the ancient legend be revealed to one outside the family. The symbol belongs to a group of high priests with dark power. We know only their name, not the men behind the name," the earl almost whispered.

"Druids," Thomas said.

"Yes, Druids! But impossible to guess!"

"From the isle of the Celts. Men now hidden among us."

"Thomas, your knowledge is frightening," the Earl of York said quickly. "Most who speak that name soon die."

Thomas smiled grimly. "That promise has already been made. Why else do I drive you to answer me all."

The Earl of York sighed. "Then I shall tell all."

He climbed down from his horse and motioned for Thomas to do the same, then gazed at the far lake of Magnus as he spoke in a flat voice.

"In our family, the ring is passed from father to eldest son, the future Earl of York. With it, these instructions: *Acknowledge the power of those behind the symbol or suffer horrible death.* And our memory is long. Three generations ago, the Earl of York refused to listen to a messenger—one whose own ring fit into the symbol engraved upon the family ring. Within weeks, worms began to consume his still living body. No doctor could cure him. Even a witch was summoned. To no avail. They say his deathbed screams echoed throughout the castle for a week. His son—my great-great-grandfather—then became the new Earl of York. When he outgrew his advisers, he took great care in acknowledging the ring which had been passed to him."

Thomas felt the chill of the earl's voice. "Acknowledge the power?"

"Yes," came the answer. "A favor asked. A command given. Rarely more than one in an earl's lifetime. Sometimes none. My great-grandfather did not receive a single request. Yet my father . . . "

The earl's voice changed from flat to sad. "My father obeyed just one command. It happened over twenty years ago. I was old enough to understand his pain. Yet he obeyed."

A thought clicked within Thomas. *Over twenty years ago . . .*

"Your father stood aside while Magnus fell," Thomas said with sudden insight. "Despite allegiance and protection promised, he let the new conquerors reign."

The Earl of York nodded.

It explained much! Thomas had sworn to his teacher, Sarah, on her deathbed that he would reconquer Magnus to avenge the brutal death of her parents, the former and rightful rulers of Magnus who had been dethroned over twenty years ago.

Then Thomas drew a deep breath as he realized the implications.

It cannot be. But he knew it was.

"Having lost it," Thomas gritted, "these Druids now demand Magnus be returned. Horrifying rituals plain to see along the march. A message for me perhaps. Or a message for you."

The Earl of York spoke slowly as he finally turned to face Thomas. His face showed the gray pallor of anguish. "Thomas, I call you friend. Yet twice along the march, in the dark of night, I was visited by one of the ring."

Thomas did not blink as he held his breath against the words he did not want to hear.

The earl's voice dropped to little more than a croak. "Each time, Thomas, I received warning to expect that payment for my family's power is soon due."

18

KATHERINE
The Midnight Messenger

Two others also traveled to Magnus, but with much less fanfare than the triumphant army returning home. These two avoided the main path through the moors, and walked slowly with caution.

Even during the warmth of daylight, the first figure remained well wrapped in black cloth. A casual observer would have aptly blamed it upon the old age so apparent by his cane and stooped shoulders, since old age often left bones aching with chill. The second figure walked tall and confident with youth. When the wind rose, it swept her long blond hair almost straight back.

They moved without pause for hours, so steadily that the casual observer would have been forced to marvel at the old man's stamina—or urgency. They finally rested at a secluded spot in the hills directly above the lake and castle of Magnus.

"I have no desire to risk you there," the old man said, pointing his cane downward at the village in the center of the lake. "But Thomas will learn both his prisoners have escaped the dungeon. That, I fear, is the bold move which marks the Druid attempt to reconquer Magnus."

"There is little risk for me," the young woman said. "My disguise served me well during my time in Magnus, and will continue to do so."

The old man arched an eyebrow barely seen in the shadows that surrounded his face. "You were a child during most of your previous time in Magnus, not a near woman now in love."

She blushed. "Is it that apparent?"

The old man shook his head. "Only in little ways. The joy on your face as we discussed a method to reach Thomas during his march to the lowland plains of battle. Your sighs during those days after our midnight meeting, when we followed the army to the Valley of Surrender. And your trembling that morning on the hillside as we awaited the outcome of his plan against the Scots."

Her blush deepened. "Thomas is worthy. I had much opportunity to watch him in Magnus. And now, perhaps my feelings will give me courage to help him as he needs."

The old man struck a slab of rock with his cane. "No!"

He looked at the now broken cane, then looked at her. His voice softened. "Please, no. Emotions are difficult to trust. Until we are certain of which side he chooses, he cannot know of you, or of the rest of us. The stakes are far too great. We risk your presence back in Magnus for the sole reason that—despite all we've done—he might become one of them. Love cannot cloud your judgment of that situation."

She ran both her hands through her hair. "You were not there," she whispered, "the day he attacked a man for insulting a poor, hideous freak. You did not see the rage in his eyes that someone so helpless should suffer. Thomas will not sell his soul. He will not be seduced by a promise of Druid power."

The old man sighed. "Beneath your words, I hear you saying something else. That you don't want to be his executioner."

19

Four trees — tall and strong — cast shadows along the main path where it became a narrow bridge of land leading across the waters of the lake to Magnus.

She approached the water alone, and instead of continuing across to the drawbridge of Magnus, walked to the base of the trees and bound her hair into a single tail, then slowly bowed to her knees out of sight of the path.

Heavy grass pressed lines into her knees through the fabric of her dress. The weight of a travel bag pressed against her hips. She cleared her mind of awareness even of the sounds of insects in afternoon sun or of the breeze which swayed the leaves above her.

There, she began to pray silently.

Lord of love, You are infinitely wise, the Creator of this universe. Please guide my steps to Your divine plan. Please give strength to Thomas, so that he chooses the path of good, and please help him find You.

A stab of fear distracted her from her contemplation. She took the fear and placed it with trust into her prayer.

Dear Father, she continued, *I am selfish to wish for his love when so much is at stake. Yet if it is Your will, please spare both our lives in the madness which might overcome Magnus. And should he choose the evil of that madness, please help me with my terrible task. In Your Son's name, our Savior, I pray. Amen.*

She stood, and for long minutes, simply stared across the water at the cold stone walls of Magnus. Despite the peace of her trust, she shivered.

Then she fumbled with the wide tongue of leather which held her travel bag closed. She reached inside and pulled loose a bundle of filthy bandages.

With practiced movements, she flipped her hair upward and pushed the long tail into a flat bundle against her head and held it there as she wrapped the cloth around her jaws, then her nose and eyes and forehead.

When she finished, only a large black hole for her mouth and two dark narrow slits for her eyes showed any degree of humanity.

Finally Katherine drew a deep breath for the strength to imprison herself in the role of a pitiful freak about to return to Magnus.

She woke in the gutter to hands reaching roughly within her blanket. Sour breath, heavy with garlic, and the odor of unwashed skin pressed down.

Katherine almost screamed in rage, then remembered her role—burned and scarred too horribly to deserve any form of kindness.

Her voice became a low begging moan instead.

"Awake? Bad luck for you!" From the darkness, a broad hand loomed to block out the light of the stars, and the blow that followed shot white flashes through her closed eyes. Her left cheek swelled immediately tight.

Katherine bit back a yelp of pain and resigned herself to being robbed of what little she owned.

Another voice interrupted the figure above her.

"My good man," it called cheerfully from just down the street, "you show kindness to assist strangers during this dangerous time of night. Here, now, let me help you get this poor woman from the gutters."

"Eh?"

The voice from behind its candle moved closer. "And probably not a moment too soon. Why, any common gutter thief might have swooped in like a pest-ridden vulture. And then where would this poor woman be?"

The startled man above Katherine swore under his breath, then fled.

She drew herself upright into a sitting position, and hugged her knees. Through the narrow slits of the constricting bandages, it was difficult to see her rescuer as he approached. It was easy, however, to hear his warm chuckle.

"Like a rat scurrying away from a torch. And with not a shred of good humor."

The candle flared and moved downward with the man's slow stooping motion. Katherine, still wrapped and hidden in a thin blanket, flinched at his touch.

"Come, my child," the voice said. "I mean you no harm. My name is Gervase. I will bring you to the church where you will be fed and kept warm."

"I have no money," Katherine replied. "Surely that must be obvious at my choice of accommodation."

Another warm chuckle. "You are a stranger here."

"No, I—"

"Otherwise, you would know the Lord of Magnus provides a

generous allowance to the church for the purpose of sheltering those in need."

His hand found her elbow and guided her to her feet.

She could not see his face behind the candle. But she heard his gasp as he pushed aside the blanket which covered her face.

That familiar sound tore at her heart. It reminded her again of the nightmare of living the life of a freak. Freedom from that life—traveling with the old man and watching the joy in his eyes as he drank in the youth and beauty of her uncovered face—had been so precious after years imprisoned beneath the filthy bandage. And for a moment, she could not sponge away bitterness inside.

"Horror?" she mocked his gasp. "You were expecting an angel perhaps?"

Long silence. Then words she would never forget. "Not horror, my child. Surprised relief. Thomas of Magnus has spoken to me often of his friend Katherine. It will give him great joy to see you."

20

Katherine woke again to the touch of hands. These ones, however, were gentle, and plucked at the bandages on her face.

"No!" Her terror was real—not acted as so much of her life beneath bandages had been.

The servant woman misunderstood the reason for that terror. "Shhh, my child. Thomas has instructed you be bathed and given fresh wraps and new clothing."

"No!" Katherine clutched the servant woman's wrists. "My face!"

"Hush, little one. You shall not be mocked in the lord's home."

Katherine did not have time to appreciate the irony—after a lifetime of abuse, kindness itself finally threatened her. *Should those of the darkness discover she had been among them all these years . . .*

Katherine pushed herself into an upright position. "Please, m'lady. Lead me to the bath. Leave the fresh wrap nearby. But I beg of you, grant me the solace of privacy. To inflict my face upon others . . . "

The servant woman responded to the urgency in Katherine's plea with a compassion that filled her eyes with tears.

"Of course," the servant woman said softly.

Katherine let strong calloused hands guide her from the warmth of the bed. Before she could barely notice the coldness of the floor, the servant woman stooped and fitted on her feet slippers of sheepskin.

As Katherine relaxed, and turned to accept help into the offered robe, she smothered a cry of delighted surprise. The previous night had been too dark for her to see her new sleeping quarters in the castle. What she saw explained why sleep had been so sound.

Her bed was huge, and canopied with veils of netting. Her mattress of straw—what luxury!—hung from the canopy on rope suspenders. The mattress was covered with linen sheets, and blankets of wool and fur. Feather-stuffed pillows too!

Such softness of sleep. Such softness of robe against her skin. Katherine suddenly became uncomfortably aware of how she must appear to a servant accustomed to awaking royalty instead.

Katherine's arms and legs were smeared with grease and dirt. The pile of clothes beside her was little more than torn rags. And, in the cool freshness of the room, she suddenly became aware of the stink of the streets upon her body.

She faltered slightly.

The servant woman ignored that.

"Come, m'lady," the woman said. "Your bath awaits. And you shall greet Thomas of Magnus like a queen."

He appears so serious, she thought. *Already, the weight of his power bends him.*

So she began her visit with an awkward bow. Katherine forced herself to remember she was beneath bandages—not a midnight messenger able to boldly show her face—and began to speak as she finished her curtsey. "You overwhelm me with these gifts of . . ."

Thomas frowned and shook his head slightly.

Katherine stopped.

Thomas stared straight ahead, every regal inch of his seated body the lord of an earldom. Behind Katherine, each side of the huge double wooden door slowly swung closed under the guidance of the sentries just outside the room.

The doors thudded shut.

Thomas let out a great sigh.

"They seem to prefer it when I am solemn," he grinned. "Apparently lords are not allowed to have fun. Especially when dispensing wisdom and justice from this very chair."

Thomas stepped down lightly.

"Katherine, you've returned." He knelt, took one of her hands, and kissed the back of it. He stood and placed both his hands on her shoulders. "I missed our conversations."

Katherine smiled beneath her bandages. *To go from formidable man to a sweet boyishness in such a short time. Not bragging about the Valley of Surrender. Not boasting of his new wealth. But to spend effort setting me—a person he believes to be a freak—at ease. It would not be difficult to remain in love with such a person.*

She, of course, kept those thoughts to herself. Instead, she replied, "Thank you, m'lord."

"M'lord! Not 'Thomas'? After you rescued me from the dungeon? After you made it possible to conquer the walls of Magnus? You gravely disappoint me with such an insult."

Grave disappointment, however, did not show on his face. Only warmth.

Would that I could tear these bandages from my face, Katherine thought. *Only to watch his eyes and hope he smiles to recognize me.*

She tried to keep the conversation safe so that nothing in her actions might betray her thoughts. "How fares that rascal Tiny John? Or the knight Sir William?"

A complex expression crossed Thomas' face—a mixture of frown and smile.

"Tiny John still entertains us all," Thomas told her as the smile triumphed.

The smile then lost to the frown and darkened. "The knight bid farewell much too soon after Magnus was conquered. There was much about him which cannot be explained."

He tried a half smile in her direction. "Much also is a mystery to me here in Magnus. Perhaps you have not heard. I left Magnus to battle the Scots. During my absence, two prisoners escaped—including the evil man Geoffrey who purchased you as a slave when he became a candlemaker. Impossible that they could escape without help from someone within Magnus. I feel there is no one here I can trust."

He looked at her strangely. "Even your disappearance the night we conquered Magnus . . ."

Katherine bowed her head. "Thomas—"

"No," he said as if coming to a quick decision. "I was not seeking an explanation. You, of anyone, assisted me to this position. I am happy that you have returned. Furthermore, urgent matters press upon me."

"Oh?"

"Strange evil generated by an ancient circle of high priests known as Druids. And worse."

Thomas stared into space. "News has reached me. The Earl of York now leads an army into the moors. His destination is Magnus."

"**As you know,**" Thomas said, "when I first arrived in Magnus, the former lord, Ranulf Pembroke, had me arrested and thrown into the dungeon because of the deaths of four monks. My explanation to you was truth. They had killed themselves by eating the food meant for me, food they themselves had poisoned in an effort to murder me."

Katherine nodded. It was a story Thomas had told her during his long spell in the dungeon—a spell which she had used to visit him each day for hours of conversation.

Thomas responded to her nod by starting to pace back and forth across the room. Brows furrowed, hands clenched behind his back, and royal purple cloak across broad shoulders.

"After Lord Pembroke fled in defeat," he continued while pacing, "all in Magnus accepted that the charges of murder had been false, merely an excuse to imprison me and the knight."

Katherine nodded again.

"Yet," Thomas said, "messengers now bring me word that the Earl of York has sworn an oath of justice, that he is determined to overthrow Magnus and execute me for those same murders."

"That is an impossible task!" Katherine finally spoke. "You are lord within these walls. Over hundreds of years, Magnus has never been taken by force alone."

"Only by treachery," Thomas agreed. "Or—as I did—with the help of the people of Magnus."

"So," Katherine asked quietly, "why does the worry fill your face?"

"A prolonged siege will do neither side any good," he answered, "and another matter, more subtle, also disturbs me."

Katherine waited. She was grateful that her old bandages had been changed to new, because even so, it was hardly possible to bear her prison of freakishness while near Thomas.

"There was enough time during the march to the battle against the Scots for the Earl of York to accuse me of murder. There was enough time then for him to arrest me. Why did he not?"

"Because his son was being held captive as a guarantee of your safety?" Katherine asked.

Thomas glanced at her briefly, then shook off a strange expression.

"No," he said a moment later. "If the charges were as true as the Earl of York obviously now believes, no one inside Magnus would have harmed his son to protect a murderer."

Long silence.

"Hadn't the Earl of York heard of the deaths before the march?" Katherine started.

"That is what puzzles me. If so, why suddenly decide to act upon them later?" Thomas stopped pacing and stared directly at Katherine.

"However," he said, "the monastery of my childhood was obscure, and me as an orphan more so. Thus, it is easier to think that the Earl of York had not heard of the deaths." Thomas frowned. "Why then did the former Lord of Magnus—here in the isolated moors—know of those deaths soon enough to cast me into the dungeon, while others in power remained uninformed until much later?"

The chamber was so narrow and tight that Katherine was forced to stand ramrod straight. Even so, the stone of the walls pressed painfully against her knees and elbows.

She had stood like that, fighting cramps of pain, in eight-hour stretches each of the previous two days. It did not help that, in the tight confines of darkness and ancient stone, the slightest movement chafed her bandages against her face.

Red raw skin and rigid muscles, then, was the price she paid to spy on Thomas.

Necessity of concealment made the chamber so small, for there was no other way it could be hidden in a hollowed portion of the thick rear wall of the throne room. Tiny vents in the cracks of stone—at a height barely above Katherine's waist and invisible to anyone inside the room—brought air upward into the space.

The vents did not allow light into the chamber, only sound, carried so perfectly that any word spoken above a whisper reached Katherine's ears.

She had no fear of being detected. Whenever Thomas left the throne room, she abandoned the hiding spot, with enough time to return to her bed chamber to clean away the dirt smudged into her by the walls before he might send a maid to invite her for conversation or a meal.

And, as the old man had instructed before sending her back to Magnus, the entrance to the chamber was fifty feet away, hidden in the recesses of a little-used hallway. To slip in or out, she need simply stand in the recess until enough quietness had convinced her that entry or exit was safe.

More difficult, however, was the twisting blackness of the tunnel which led through the thick castle walls to the chamber behind the throne room. More than once, she had felt the slight crunch of stepping on the fur and bones of long dead and dusty dry mice and—she shuddered—bats. Her first time through, two days earlier, had been a gagging passage past cobwebs that brushed her eyelashes in the darkness with no warning and clung to her like lace.

Remember the old man and his instructions, she told herself as yet another cramp bit into her left thigh. *This is a duty that we have performed for generations.*

Two days of petitions and complaints. Two days of the slowly considered words given in return by the earl, Thomas of Magnus. Two days of exquisite torture, listening and loving more the man who might never discover the secret of her hidden face. But not once did she hear the expected Druid messenger.

Yet the Druid would arrive. The old man had so promised, and the old man was never wrong.

Katherine snapped herself away from her thoughts, and listened to another verdict, delivered so crystal clear into the chamber.

"No, Gervase, there will not be any more money supplied from the treasury for church charity."

"My lord?"

His sigh reached her with equal clarity. "Gervase, much as you pretend surprise, you expected that decision from me. You know—as I do—that many are now tempted to forsake work for the easiness of charity meals and sound sleep."

Gervase chuckled. "What do you propose? Every day, one or two more appear at the church doorstep."

"Get the father to deliver long sermons. Ones which must be

heard before the meals arrive."

Laughter from both.

Then a more sober tone from Thomas. "Find work on the church building or its grounds," he said. "Any work. Let those who are able contribute long hours, enough so that it is more profitable for them to seek employment elsewhere. You will soon discover who is truly needy."

"Excellent," Gervase said. "I look forward to our evening walk and discussion. Maybe you shall tell me more about Katherine."

In the chamber, Katherine's ears began to burn from embarrassment. It was one thing to spy for noble purposes, another to listen to a private conversation. Yet she found herself straining to catch every word.

"Yes. Katherine. I have questions . . ."

What . . . did he mean . . . ?

She was given no time to ponder.

"M'lord. One waits here outside," a sentry called into the throne room.

Katherine, of course, could only imagine the silent good-bye salutes between Thomas and Gervase, and the voice she heard moments later sent an instinctive fear deep inside her.

"Thomas of Magnus." Not a question, but almost a sneer. The voice was modulated, and had no coarse accent of an uneducated peasant.

"Most extend courtesy with a bow," Thomas replied, immediately cold.

"I will not prolong this through pretense," the voice replied. "I am here to discuss your future."

A pause. Then the voice spoke quickly. "Don't! You draw breath to call for a guard, but if you do, you will never learn the secrets of this symbol, nor of Magnus."

The Druid messenger.

Katherine no longer felt the ache of stiff limbs. She no longer noticed the wraps of cloth which muffled her breath. Every nerve tingled to listen further.

"You have two minutes," Thomas replied.

"No," came the now soft and triumphant voice. "I have as long as I like. Dread curiousity is plain to read on your face."

"Your time slips away as you speak. What is your message?"

The sneering voice came like a soft caress. "The message is simple. Join our circle, remain earl and gain great power beyond comprehension. Or deny us and lose Magnus."

2 2

"**Why should I not** have you seized and executed?" Thomas asked after a long silence.

"For the same reason that you still live. After all, we have a thousand ways to kill you. An adder perhaps—that deadly snake—slipped into your bedsheets as you sleep. Undetectable poisons, a dagger in the heart. You still live, Thomas, because your death does not serve our purpose. My death would not serve yours."

"No?" Thomas asked.

"No. You and I are merely representatives. Your death only ends your life. It does not return to us the power over the people of Magnus, who—before your arrival—were sheep to be handled at our whims."

Short silence. Then from Thomas, "And you represent?" He said it with too much urgency.

The messenger laughed. A cruel sound to Katherine in her hiding spot. "Druids. The true masters of Magnus for centuries."

"Not possible," Thomas said. But Katherine heard enough of

a waver in his voice to know he did think it possible.

"Not possible?" the voice countered. "Ponder this. Magnus is an incredible fortress. A king's fortune ten times over could not pay for the construction of this castle and the protective walls. Yet to all appearances, Magnus is located far, far from the bases of power. Why go to the expense, if not for a hidden purpose?

"And," the voice moved like an arched finger slowly scratching a cat's throat, "why has Magnus existed so long without being seriously challenged by the royalty of England? The Earl of York leaves it in peace. So have the Norman kings and the Anglo-Saxons before them. Would not even a fool decide great power lies within Magnus, great enough to deflect kings for centuries?"

No! Katherine raged. *Thomas must not believe these lies!*

"Why did the former lord, Ranulf Pembroke, take Magnus by the foulest treachery?" Thomas said with hesitation. "If you speak truth, it would seem to me that your circle would control this castle's destiny."

"Of course," came the snorted reply. "That's exactly why Ranulf Pembroke was *allowed* to conquer Magnus. He was loyal to us. The earl before him . . ."

"Yes?" Thomas asked with ice in his voice.

"Don't be a child! We certainly know that his daughter Sarah raised you at that forsaken monastery. Can you not consider the possibility it was she who lied to you, not us?"

Katherine almost needed to force herself to breathe. She felt her nails bite her palms, but still did not unclench her fists.

Thomas, don't accept their lies! Please, don't force me to be your executioner! In the heartbeats that followed, Katherine agonized. Thomas did not know enough to make a decision, yet there was too great a risk in giving him the truth.

"I have considered the possibility that she lied," Thomas said finally. "And logically, there is no reason against it. I was an orphan and depended on her for much. It would be difficult for a lost child to recognize the difference between truth or false-hood."

If Katherine could have slumped in that cramped hollow, she would have. *I now wish he had never looked into my eyes,* she told herself.

"Good, good," the voice purred. "We much prefer that you choose to live as one of us. You will share the mysteries of darkness with us, and anything you wish will become yours."

"It must have a price," Thomas said, almost defeated. "The rewards may be plain to see, but loyalty has its demands."

"Thomas, Thomas," the voice chided. "We wish only one thing as a test of your commitment."

"Yes?" Now the pleading of total defeat.

"Your hidden books of knowledge. We must have them."

If he agrees, Katherine told herself, *nothing will ease the pain of my duty. Yet he cannot lead them to the books. I must force my hands to betray my love for him, and tonight he will die.*

"Go," Thomas said with sudden strength and intensity. "Go back to the isle of the Celts!"

Katherine blinked in her darkness.

"Yes!" Thomas raged. "Report back to your murdering bar-barian masters that Thomas of Magnus will not bend to those who brand the chests of innocent men."

"Yet—"

"Yet it appeared I might pledge loyalty? Only to see what it was you truly wished. Now, I shall do everything in my power to prevent you from that desire."

"Fool!" The word sounded as if it was molten iron, spat bright red from a furnace. "Magnus shall be taken from you as it was given. By the people."

"That remains to be seen," Thomas said in a steady voice.

Behind her mask of bandages, tears of relief filled Katherine's eyes.

2 3

The first howl began while Katherine and Tiny John walked the streets of Magnus. Then another, from farther away.

"Listen." Tiny John cocked his head. As usual, a grin shone bright from dirty and smudged skin. No matter how often the clucking castle servants managed to hold him motionless long enough to wipe him clean, he found a way to crawl, run, or scamper through a hole or passageway just narrow enough to make their efforts useless. It was amazing, in fact, that he had slowed down long enough to escort Katherine to the market.

"Listen to what? These dogs?" Katherine snorted. Her mind was not on the streets bustling with early morning activity, nor on Tiny John's happy prattling. A single night had passed since the Druid visitor had proclaimed his warning to Thomas, and Katherine's stomach still churned with fear. She, of anyone in Magnus, knew the power of the barbarian Druids.

Worse, the Earl of York was expected to arrive in the valley with his army sometime in midafternoon. Katherine—again of anyone in Magnus—knew Thomas faced enemies both inside and outside the fortress of Magnus.

What would be the first attack?

Then Katherine's skin prickled. *Another unearthly howl.*

Within moments, the shrieking chorus filled Magnus.

Dogs—in the streets, under carts, in sheds—all through Magnus moaned and howled and barked.

People stopped and stared around in amazement. Then in superstitious fear.

The howling grew louder and more frenzied.

An unease filled Katherine, an unease which had nothing to do with the almost supernatural noise of the dogs. She wanted to hold her head and shake away the grip of something she couldn't explain.

Now cats.

The high-pitched scream of yeowling cats gradually became plain above the yipping and howling of dogs.

All people stood where they were, frozen in awed dread. Rats scurried from dark hiding places, from the corners of market stalls, from the holes among stone walls, and in dozens of places ran headlong and uncaring across the feet of shopkeepers and market people.

Then, unbelievably, bats!

Dozens fell from the sky. A great swarm circled frantically a hundred feet above Magnus, each bat dipping and swooping a crazed dance to death.

Bats do not fly during the daytime, Katherine told herself as she struggled to accept what her eyes told her. *And they do not drop like a hailstorm of dark stones.*

Still the bats fell. Onto thatched roofs. Onto the carts of shopkeepers. Onto the dried packed dirt of the streets.

The thud of their landing bodies was lost among the howling and shrieking of cats and dogs.

And into the noise came the screams of terrified peasants.

Then, like a snuffed candle, it stopped.

The dozens of bats dropped from the sky to quiver and shake in death throes. The dogs stopped howling. The cats stopped shrieking.

And, stunned by the sudden end of noise, the terrified peasants stopped screaming.

Whispers began.

"A judgment from God," someone said.

"Yes," another said, more clearly. "We allow a murderer of monks to remain Lord of Magnus!"

"The Earl of York brings justice with his army!"

"God's judgment!"

"Yes! God's judgment upon us!"

The whispers around them in the marketplace became shouts of anger and fear.

Tiny John reached up and held Katherine's hand. She squeezed comfort in return. The boy needed it.

"We'll . . ." Her legs trembled as she hid her fear from Tiny John. She forced herself to swallow, her mouth was so dry. "We'll return immediately. Thomas must hear of this. If he hasn't been informed already."

Katherine joined Thomas along the tops of the walls.

"The Earl of York makes no effort to hide the size of his army," she observed.

"He has no need," Thomas replied. "Magnus, of course, cannot flee."

They shared silence as they watched the faraway blur of banners leading the army's approach.

Still at least two miles away, that mass of soldiers and horses was plain to see as it wound its way through the valley.

Katherine ached to tell Thomas more, to tell him that he was not alone in his struggle against the Druids. But she could not. The old man's remembered warning echoed stronger than the inner voice which instructed her to remove the bandages from her face.

Yet tonight she would slip away from Magnus and speak again to the old man.

"Will you see the Earl of York?" she asked.

Thomas shook his head. "We will deal through messengers."

Unspoken was the thought neither could avoid. *Already, division weakens Magnus within. Thomas can ill afford to leave to conduct negotiations himself.*

"Who do you trust?" Katherine asked several minutes later. "Robert of Uleran?"

"His dismay at the escape of the prisoners in my absence seemed real," Thomas said. "Upon my return, he offered his resignation. Now . . . now I have no other choice but to trust him. It is only his strong insistence that keeps many of the soldiers faithful to our cause."

Katherine shivered—despite the afternoon sun—at her memory of the uncanny events of the morning. Not a single peasant in Magnus believed any longer that Thomas was innocent of the murders of innocent monks. Not for the first time did Katherine consider the harm that a few well-placed rumors from Druid sources might cause. Yet how could they have called bats from the sky to add strength to the rumors?

She had nothing more to say, and she wanted only to place her hand on his arm. But Thomas stared with rigid anger at the approaching army.

Shortly after, the sounds of that army drifted upward to them. Grunting beasts. The slap of leather against ground as men marched in unison. And the rise of voices behind Thomas and Katherine as villagers heard of the army's progress.

When the army reached the narrow bridge of land that connected the island fortress to the land around the lake, one man, on foot, detached himself from the front of the army.

Thomas watched briefly, then spoke more to himself than to Katherine as the man walked alone slowly toward the castle.

"He holds paper rolled and sealed. I have little faith the message is a greeting of friendship."

2 4

Katherine reached the secluded grove long after the final bells of midnight had rung clearly across the valley from within Magnus. She blamed it on caution generated by the necessity to avoid an entire army camped around the lake of Magnus.

Bent and covered in shawls, more than once to get by a sentry she had had to play the role of a disoriented servant, seeking her tent in the darkness. And each time she had faced a sentry, she had gripped tightly beneath her shawl a dagger. *Nothing must keep her from the old man.*

The long walk along the valley bottom through the black of night had not been easy either. In her mind, each rustle of leaves, each sway of branches, each tiny movement was a falling bat or a scurrying rat. Before, the night had held nothing to frighten her. Now, after the horror of those brief moments in Magnus, it was difficult to recover her innocence from fear of animals.

Her nerves, however, had not prevented her from making steady progress. Step by step, tree by tree, clearing by clearing, she had moved toward the prearranged meeting place.

As always, the old man was waiting as promised.

He wasted no time with greetings. Nor in seeking identification. Only Katherine would know of this place.

"What happens in Magnus?"

She felt a brief pride that he trusted her enough to assume she succeeded in her mission. "As you foresaw," Katherine said, "those of darkness sent a messenger."

"And as *you* predicted," the old man said after some thought, "he refused to be bullied or bribed."

"Yes, but how do you know of—"

"Katherine, had you been forced to be his executioner, nothing could have hidden it in your voice. Thus, I know he is alive. And alive only because he wants no part of the Druids."

"There is more," she said, and explained the morning's happenings, and the rumbles of fear within Magnus.

The old man mused for several minutes. "Your fear is legitimate, my child. Kings—no matter what they wish to believe— rule only by the consent of the people. History is scarred by the revolutions against fools who believed otherwise. Thomas may indeed lose Magnus."

"And Thomas grieves," Katherine told the old man. "He is bewildered by the earl's declaration of war, and moreover by the earl's fierce anger. Thomas once believed they were friends as close as brothers."

Katherine explained the savage message delivered late that afternoon by scroll. *Unconditional surrender or unconditional death.* She explained too how Thomas wondered why the former Lord of Magnus had heard of the monks' deaths so much before the Earl of York had.

"It is part of their circle," the old man said. "Do not ask to know more."

The old man paused. "Then, I'm sure, it was convenient for

the Druids that only the then reigning Lord of Magnus know. Now, of course, they prefer for the Earl of York to know as well. It will be much easier for the Druids if the Earl of York fights their battle in misguided pursuit of justice."

Katherine nodded. "The dogs. The cats. Bats falling dead from the sky. Now that the people within Magnus believe justice must be served against Thomas, he may lose his lordship the same way he gained it."

"I catch doubt of his innocence even in your voice, child."

Katherine sighed. "Slight doubts only. How could our enemies be capable of calling bats to hurl themselves down from the sky?"

"It is a question not easily answered," the old man agreed. "Let me think."

Katherine knew better than to speak again.

The old man then sat cross-legged and arranged his mantle over him to fend off the cold night air.

Katherine waited. And knew too well how long that wait might be. She waited as the cold seeped into her. She waited as her legs, tired from her journey, grew to feel soreness even more. She waited in silence broken only by distant muttering of owls and the light skipping of mice across leaves.

Not until the gray fingers of false dawn reached into the valley did the old man stir.

When he finally spoke, it was a question.

"Close your eyes," he said to Katherine. "Do you recall if you saw the smoke of a fire as the creatures howled in Magnus?"

She did as instructed. Eyes closed lightly, at first she saw in her memory only the frantic movement of bats against the morning sky. Then, dimly, something snagged in her memory because it did not belong against that sky.

"Yes," she said. "Smoke from the bell tower of the church!"

The old man let out held breath. "And you say you felt like

shaking your head free from a grip you can't explain."

Katherine nodded. In the cold dawn, slight wisps rose white from her mouth with the rise and fall of her chest. Even in summer, the high moors and valleys could not escape chill.

Did she imagine that a smile appeared in the shadows of his cowl?

He spoke slowly in his low rasping tones. "Speak to Thomas tonight. As yourself, unencumbered with bandages. If he has courage, he can defeat the Druids."

25

She hoped for, watched for—and with thudding heart—saw the startled flare of recognition in his eyes.

"You!"

"Yes, Thomas. I bring greetings from an old man. One saddened to hear of your troubles."

"You! Impossible! Soldiers are posted at every turret."

Katherine repeated her greetings—cool on the outside, glad inside that her sudden presence had shocked him into not hearing her first words.

They stood—nearly in the same positions as a day earlier when Katherine had posed as a bandaged freak—on the outside walls of Magnus. Fifty yards farther along the top of the wall a soldier stood posted at a square stone turret. Fifty yards farther behind, the same thing.

Below and across the water were campfires of the sieging army, so close they heard the pop and so close they saw the sparks whenever a log exploded in the heat.

Thomas groaned and laughed in the same sound.

"Why must I be tortured so? Is it not enough that Magnus rumbles with rebellion? That the most powerful earl in north Britain camps on my doorstep? That the sorcery of Druids threatens? That you haunt my dreams?"

His dreams are haunted.

The groan deepened. "And with all of that, you place in front of me the never-ending mystery of the old man."

He shook his head, and in light joking tones said, "I pray thee tell me all."

"I cannot," she said. *Although I wish to,* she thought.

"For example," he said, "tell me how you arrived here, within Magnus during a siege, on these walls during the night?"

She shook her head.

"Perhaps why you and the old man dog my footsteps?"

She shook her head.

"The identity of the old man?"

Another shake.

"The mission he wishes me to pursue?"

Again, Katherine shook her head silently.

In one quick, almost angry motion, he stepped across the space between them, and pulled her close and kissed her squarely on the lips. Then he pushed her away.

"And if you enjoyed that."

Katherine's first response—and one too immediate to stop—was to slap him hard—open palm against open face—for taking such action without permission or invitation. Her second response was regret at the first response.

A woman should not value lightly her first kiss, she thought. *Not if it is one never to be forgotten.*

"M'lord?" One of the sentries had heard the noise of the slap.

Katherine could not help but giggle. "I didn't intend to hit *that* hard," she whispered.

"It's nothing," Thomas called back to the sentry. Then to

Katherine, "Punishment justly deserved."

They stared at each other. Thoughts and impressions crowded Katherine's mind. His now grave and steady eyes, clearly seen in the light of the moon. The skin which had tightened across cheekbones from worry. His features—somehow mature, yet not far from boyhood.

Stop, she told herself. *It is duty which takes you here.*

So she spoke. "You talk of rebellion within Magnus, of the army across the water, and of the sorcery of Druids."

Thomas nodded without taking his eyes away from hers.

Will he have the courage?

She plunged ahead. "The old man wishes for me to tell you that there is a way to overcome all three."

He must have the courage.

"How is that?" Thomas asked.

She paused before answering, then said, "Ask for God's judgment. Trial by ordeal."

2 6

Katherine, Thomas, Robert of Uleran, and Tiny John stood and waited at the end of the drawbridge.

At the other end of the narrow strip of land that reached the shore of the lake, the Earl of York and three soldiers began to move toward them.

"Are you sure they'll not run us through with those great swords?" Tiny John asked, not for the first time that morning.

"Yes," Katherine whispered. "The earl will not risk losing honor by dealing treachery. Not after Thomas requested a meeting such as this."

Her answer did not stop Tiny John from fidgeting as the Earl of York moved closer.

Beside her, Thomas and Robert of Uleran stared straight ahead. Each wore a long cloak of the finest material in Magnus—it was not a time to appear humble.

For Katherine, the Earl of York's march across the land bridge seemed to take forever. How badly she wanted it to still be the previous night, with Thomas listening so carefully to her words, half his attention on her face, the other half to the instructions from the old man. How badly she wanted it to be that single moment of farewell, with the awkwardness of Thomas not daring to hold her, yet hoping she would not disappear again.

And how badly she wanted to be free of the bandages which now disguised her from Thomas.

The Earl of York was now close enough for Katherine to observe the anger set in the clenched muscles of his face.

She heard that anger moments later.

"What is it that you want, you craven cur of yellow cowardice?"

A quick, surprised intake of breath from Thomas.

"An explanation perhaps, of this sudden hatred," Thomas said shortly after. "I understand—if you truly believe me guilty of those murders—that duty forces you to lay siege. But you called me brother once. Surely that—"

"Treacherous vulture. Waste no charm on me," the earl said in thunderous tones. "Were it not for honor, I would cleave you in two where you stand. You called me here for discussion. Do it quickly, so that I may refuse your request and return to the important matter of bringing destruction to Magnus."

Thomas stiffened visibly and he kept his voice level and polite. "I ask then for a chance to prove my innocence."

"Surrender the castle then. Submit to a trial."

Thomas shook his head. "I ask for trial by ordeal."

The Earl of York gaped at him. "Ordeal!"

That too had been Katherine's reaction to the old man's instructions.

"Ordeal!" the Earl of York repeated, showing for the first time emotion other than anger. "The church outlawed such trials more than a hundred years ago."

"Nonetheless," Thomas said, "I wish to prove to you and to the people of Magnus that I am innocent."

The earl rubbed his chin in thought. "Tell me, shall we bind you and throw you into the lake?"

That had been, as Katherine knew, one of the most common ways of establishing guilt. Bound, and often weighted with stones, a person was thrown into deep water. If he or she did not drown, innocence was declared.

"Not by water," Thomas said. "Nor by fire."

Some chose the hot iron. The defendant was forced to pick up an iron weight, still glowing from the forge. If, after three days in bandages, the burns had healed, it was taken as a sign of innocence.

"What then?" the Earl of York demanded. "How are we to believe you are innocent?"

"Tomorrow, I will stand alone on this narrow strip of land," Thomas said. "Stampede toward me twenty of the strongest and largest bulls you can find. If I turn and run, or if I am crushed and trampled, then you may have Magnus."

27

Katherine stood among the great crowd at the base of the castle.

For once, she was grateful for the bandages around her face. It hid her ironic smile to notice the stale sweat stench of the men and women hemmed against her—several days of luxurious baths during castle living had spoiled her.

She was in the crowd because she wanted to hear and watch Thomas, and there was no way for her to remain beside him as he addressed the people from atop the castle stairs.

When he appeared, the rustling undercurrents of speculation immediately stopped. Thomas held complete attention.

"People of Magnus," Thomas began, "today I face death."

Whispered and excited chattering.

Thomas held up his hand for silence. He wore only simple clothes. A brown cloak. No jewelry.

"Because of you I undergo trial by ordeal. Magnus can withstand any siege, but only with your support. Some of you have chosen to believe I am guilty of the charges laid against me. Today, then, I prove my innocence so that Magnus might stand."

Now his face darkened, the face of nobility angered. "And I tell you now, dogs will howl and bats will fall from the sky at the injustice of false accusations."

Thomas said nothing more. He spun on his heel and marched back into the castle.

Surely he feels fear.

From Katherine's viewpoint among the hundreds of men and women of Magnus lined along the top of the fortress wall, Thomas appeared small and lost to be standing alone halfway across the land bridge.

Thomas stood completely still and faced the opposing army. Between them, and where the land bridge joined the shore of the lake, a hastily constructed pen—made from logs roped together—held huge and restless bulls. From the castle wall, they seemed dark and evil.

Katherine frowned. Why a heap of dried bushes at the back end of that pen?

The collective tension of spectators began to fill her too.

Dear God, she prayed, *let the old man be correct in his calculations.*

Soldiers moved to the front of the pen.

A sigh from the crowd along the fortress wall, like the wind that swept down the valley hills across them.

Thomas crossed his arms, and moved his feet apart slightly, as if bracing himself.

If he turns and runs, he declares his guilt. Yet how can he remain there as the bulls charge?

A sudden muttering took Katherine from her thoughts. She looked beyond Thomas, and understood immediately.

The bush at the rear of the pen! Soldiers with torches! They meant to drive the bulls into a frenzy with fire!

The vulnerable figure that was Thomas remained planted. Katherine fought unexplainable tears.

Within moments, the dried bush crackled, and high flames were plain to see from the castle walls.

Screamed bellows of rage filled the air as the massive bulls began to push forward against the gate. Monstrous dark silhouettes rose from the rear and struggled to climb those in front as the fire surged higher and higher.

Then, just as the pen itself bulged outward from the strain of tons upon tons of heavy muscle in panic, the soldiers slashed the rope which held the gate shut.

Bulls exploded forward in a massed charge.

Fifty yards away, Thomas waited.

Does he cry for help? Katherine could not watch. Neither could she close her eyes. Not with the thunder that pounded the earth. Not with the bellowed terror and fury and roar of violence of churning hooves and razor-sharp horns bearing down on him like a black storm of hatred.

Thirty-five yards away, Thomas waited.

Men and women around Katherine began to scream.

Still, he did not move.

Twenty-five yards. Then twenty.

One more heartbeat and the gap had closed to fifteen yards.

Screams grew louder.

Then the unbelievable.

The lead bulls swerved, plunged into the water on either side of Thomas. Within moments, even as the bellows of rage drowned out the screams atop the castle walls, the bulls parted as they threw themselves away from the tiny figure in front of them.

Katherine slumped.

It was over.

No bull remained on land. Each swam strongly for the nearest shore.

Another sigh from the crowd atop the castle's walls. But before excited talk could begin, the first of the bulls reached shore. As it landed and took its first steps, it roared with renewed rage and bolted away from the cautiously approaching soldiers.

Small saplings snapped as it charged and bucked and bellowed through the trees lining the shore, through the empty tents and campfires beyond, and finally to the open land.

Each bull did the same as it reached land, and soldiers fled in all directions.

And behind the people, dogs started to howl in the streets. The men and women of Magnus turned in time to see bats swooping and rising in panic in bright sunshine until, moments later, the first one fell to earth.

2 8

Katherine did not see Thomas anywhere on the streets of Magnus during the celebration which traditionally followed the end of a siege. Merchants and shopkeepers—normally cheap to the point of meanness—poured wine for the lowliest of peasants, and freely shared the best cakes and freshest meats.

Around her was joyful song—much of it off-key because of the wine—and the vibrant plucked tunes of six-stringed lutes and the jangle of tambourines.

People danced and hugged each other as long-lost brothers, even the most bitter of neighbors. Today, the threat of death had vanished, and their lord, Thomas of Magnus, had been proven innocent. How could they have ever doubted?

Only the most cynical would have observed that much of the celebration was desperation. Not a single person in Magnus wanted to remember the uncanny howling of dogs and the death of bats that had followed Thomas' trial by ordeal. No, that was something to be banished from memory, something that, if possible, they all would pretend had never happened.

Katherine moved aimlessly from street to street. Never, of course, in her life as a freak in Magnus had she felt like she belonged. This celebration was no different. Few offered her cakes, few offered her wine, and no one took her hand to dance. *Did it matter?* She wondered. All those years of loneliness, years served as duty for a greater cause. She thought she had become accustomed to the cruelty of people who judged merely by appearance.

Yet today, the pain drove past the cold walls around her heart. Because of Thomas. Because she could remember not wearing the bandages. Like a bird freed from its cage, then imprisoned again, she longed to fly.

Now, walking along the streets and among the crowds, thinking of Thomas darkened her usual loneliness.

Yes, Thomas had proven his courage. Yes, Thomas had defeated the Druid attempt at rebellion within Magnus. And yes, Thomas had also turned away the most powerful earl in the north.

But the Druids had not been completely conquered. As well, the Earl of York had departed as a sworn enemy—a mystery which she knew both bewildered and tormented Thomas. Magnus was not free from danger.

Katherine frowned to herself, not that—she realized—it was necessary to hide that frown beneath her bandages. She was disappointed in her selfishness. So much was at stake. Her duty to the old man proved it day after day. Yet, she could barely look beyond her feelings—a frustrating ache—and the insane desire to rip from her face the bandages which hid her from Thomas.

She sighed, remembering the old man's instructions. *Until we are certain of which side he chooses, he cannot know of you, or of the rest of us. The stakes are far too great. We risk your presence back in Magnus for the sole reason that—despite all we've done—he might become one of them. Love cannot cloud your judgment of that situation.*

Head down and lost in her thoughts, Katherine did not see Gervase until he clapped a friendly hand upon her shoulder.

"Dear friend," he said. "Thomas wishes you to join him."

"The Roman caltrops worked as the old man predicted," Thomas said as greeting. He stood beside the large chair in his throne room, and did not even wait for the guard to close the large doors.

Thomas trusts me enough to reveal how he survived the charge of the bulls?

Katherine kept her voice calm. Only the two of them in the room. She could bluff. "Predicted? Forgive my ignorance, m'lord." After all, the person behind the bandages should have no understanding of caltrops, or of an old man.

"Katherine," Thomas chided. "Caltrops. Small sharp spikes. Hundreds of years ago, Roman soldiers used to scatter them on the ground to break up cavalry charges. Certainly you remember. After all, the old man gave you instructions for me. 'Go the night before and seed the earth with the spikes. Bulls are not shod with iron. The spikes will pierce their feet and drive them into the water.' "

"M'lord?"

Behind her bandage, beads of sweat began to form on Katherine's face.

"Katherine . . . " He used patient exasperation, a parent humoring a dull child. "We are friends, remember? You need not keep the pretense. After all, you're the one who told me how to bring dogs to a frenzy. How to force bats to their deaths in daylight."

"M'lord."

"Come here," Thomas said sharply.

Katherine did not move. Not with legs frozen in shock.

So Thomas stepped toward her. He lifted a hand to her bandaged face.

"No!" she cried. "You cannot shed light upon my face! It is too hideous."

Thomas dropped his hand. "These are your choices. Unwrap it yourself. Let me unwrap it. Or, if you struggle, the guards will be called to hold you down. They will also be witnesses . . . something I'll wager you do not wish."

Impossible he should have guessed her identity.

Katherine whimpered, something she had learned to do well over the years. "M'lord . . . the humiliation. How can you force me to—"

"I shall count to three. Then I call the guards."

He stared at her, cold and serious.

Katherine firmed her chin. "I shall do it myself."

It seemed a dream, to be within Magnus and finally removing the hated mask. Wrap by wrap, she removed the cloth around her face. When she finished, she shook her hair free. And waited, defiant.

"You did that in the moonlight once," Thomas said with wonder in his voice. "You loosed your hair and gazed at me directly thus. I shall never forget."

Confusion. Do I feel anger or relief? She showed neither. Merely waited.

"Please," Thomas said, gentle. "Sit and talk."

She remained standing. "How long did you know?"

He shook his head. "How long did I *suspect.* Since you arrived back as Katherine beneath those bandages. That is your name? Katherine?"

She nodded. He smiled.

He is not raging at the deception?

"Your disappearance the night after I conquered Magnus," Thomas began. "At first, I thought the soldiers had killed you and hidden the body. There could be no other explanation. After all, I had promised you anything if Magnus was won."

I remember that well, Katherine thought. *I remember wishing for something you could never give to a freak behind bandages, not with Isabelle in your heart.*

"When you returned—unharmed—so much later, I could not think of a reason why you would remain away from Magnus so long, knowing I had conquered it. But I did not want to ask."

"Yes," Katherine said, "I remember you cut me short when I tried to explain."

"I had been lied to already," Thomas said, "by someone whose beauty nearly matches yours."

"Isabelle. You thought of her often while waiting in the dungeon."

"I did," Thomas said. "She was a lesson well learned. Mere admiration of beauty does not make love. I confess, however, to have learned feelings for you when you were the Katherine behind the mask . . . "

He stopped himself and his voice faltered slightly. "There was a strangeness when we first met that night along the march, the night I first saw your face. As if we had memories to share. I want to trust you, and that feeling itself is something I cannot trust. So I watched you carefully for deception."

"Thomas—"

He did not let her finish. "There was your unexplained entrance into Magnus. Since the night you disappeared, all guards at the drawbridge had instructions to watch for one whose face was hidden by bandages. I hoped always for your return. Yet, when you finally arrived, no guard noticed. Thus, I was forced to conclude you had entered as you are now. Unmasked."

Katherine did not protest. *Better that he did not know the truth.*

"So," Thomas said, "I pretended trust. I wanted to learn more about you, and playing the fool seemed the best way. The dungeon, as you know, had little effect in getting the truth from Isabelle. I thought honey would work better than vinegar."

He held up a hand to forestall her reply. "Finally," Thomas said, "you, as the midnight messenger, were able to appear within Magnus even during a siege. Since it would be impossible for you to leave or enter with an army camped around us, I decided you had been here before the siege began. As, of course, Katherine."

Once again, she managed not to betray her thoughts. *He must not know the truth about my method of escape, or my visit, then, to the old man during the siege.*

So she said, "You are not filled with anger at my deception."

Thomas smiled. "Not yet."

2 9

Katherine felt a skip in her chest. *Not yet.*

Sadness and joy tinged his smile as he spoke again.

"Katherine," he said. "I learned to know you as the one be-hind the mask long before you spellbound me beneath a mid-night moon. You are courageous, you love truth, you love God. And you brought me instructions which saved Magnus. It is much easier to believe you are not an enemy."

"I am not," she said quickly. "How can I convince you?"

"Tell me about the old man. Tell me about the mission he has placed upon my shoulders. Tell me why you endured endless years in the horror of disguise." His voice grew urgent, almost passionate. "Tell me the secret of Magnus!"

Many long moments of silence. Many long moments of want-ing to trust, wanting to tell him everything.

But she could not. There was the old man and his instruc-tions. *Love cannot cloud your judgment of that situation.* And too much was at stake.

Finally, and very slowly, she shook her head. "I cannot."

Thomas sighed. "As I thought. Even now, I cannot find anger."

She moved toward him and placed a hand on his arm. "Please . . ."

"No," he said with sadness. "I know so little. All I can cling to is the memory of someone who gave me the key to Magnus, and the reason to conquer. More important to her than winning Magnus, was a treasure of . . . of . . ."

Books, Katherine thought. *Knowledge in an age of darkness.*

"Books," Thomas said. "You know that because I told you the night I conquered Magnus. It is a mistake I now regret."

"Regret?"

"I should have kept my secret. How am I to know you are not one of the Druids? Perhaps, by appearing to help save me from the earl, you deceive me into revealing what the Druids want most."

"Thomas, no!"

Still sadness as he spoke. "No? The Druids first caused dogs to howl unnaturally with the rubbing of crystal glass into sounds so high pitched the animals writhed in torment. The Druids first caused bats to leave their roosts by lighting a fire beneath, and poisoning them with the smoke of yew branches thrown on that fire. Then you reveal to me those secrets so that by using the same methods, I can cause the villagers to believe in my innocence once again."

"No!" she pleaded again.

"How is it then you know what the Druids do? Even astronomy, as the old man proved with his trickery at the gallows. If you are not Druids, who are you?"

That was the question she wanted to answer. More than anything she wanted to answer it. But she could not.

Tears streamed shiny down her cheeks as she shook her head again.

"I am sorry, m'lady," Thomas said. He lifted her hand from his arm, then took some of her hair and wiped her face of tears. "I cannot trust you. This battle—whatever it might be—I fight alone."

His touch, she thought and ached. *Kind. His eyes. Now distant.*

He lifted her chin with a finger. "Know this, Katherine. The God of which you spoke. He let me find Him."

Katherine opened her mouth to ask. He placed his finger against her lips.

"No more," he said. "Remember, I shall not forget you as the Katherine—the real Katherine—who comforted me in the depths of a dungeon and told me of God. Because of her, the person you were beneath those bandages, I cannot and shall not hold you here against your will."

He turned away from her as he spoke his final words. "Please depart Magnus."

The *Winds of Light* continues . . .

In *The Legend of Burning Water*, Thomas faces a deadly threat from enemies within the church itself—imposters taking power from the legendary Holy Grail of King Arthur's Round Table of Knights. Unable to fight with sword or knowledge, he is forced into desperate action, guided by strangers he dare not trust, strangers who know all of the truth behind Magnus.

HISTORICAL NOTES

Readers may find it of interest that in the times in which the Winds of Light series is set, children were considered adults much earlier than now. By church law, for example, a bride had to be at least twelve, a bridegroom fourteen. (This suggests that upon occasion, marriage occurred at an even earlier age!)

It is not so unusual then to think of Thomas of Magnus becoming a leader by the age of 14; many would already consider him a man simply because of his age. Moreover, other "men" also became leaders at remarkably young ages during those times. King Richard II, for example, was only 14 years old when he rode out to face the leaders of the Peasants' Revolt in 1381.

Here are more historical notes on *Barbarians from the Isle:*

Chapter One
Even by the year A.D. 1312, **York** was already an ancient and major center in northwestern England. Located roughly 18 miles south of Helmsley—the site of the hanging—York was an outpost for Roman soldiers 1,250 years before the times in which

Thomas of Magnus lived. Any single man given jurisdiction over this city and surrounding area would have had considerable power.

Chapter Two

The Scots posed a serious threat to the English King Edward II, who reigned from 1307 to 1327. Robert Bruce, crowned King of Scotland in 1306, nearly lost Scotland in his first battles against the English because of the leadership of Edward II's father, King Edward I. When Edward I died in July 1307, however, Robert Bruce was able to oppose the weaker Edward II, and began a series of successful battles. In the years 1312 to 1314, Robert Bruce defeated a series of English strongholds and the restoration of English power in Scotland became an impossibility. In 1318, the Scots finally captured the castle of Berwick on the English border and from there were easily able to raid as far south as the Yorkshire area.

Chapter Six

It may be of interest to note that in A.D. 1297, Edward I's royal army in Flanders consisted of 7,810 foot soldiers and 895 calvary, of which only 140 were knights.

At that time, the knight carried shield, lance, and sword into battle. His basic armor was a suit of chain mail, reinforced with steel plates at the knees and shoulders. During the 1300s, plating gradually began to replace chain mail as protection, until eventually, in the 1400s, knights were slow and heavy with complete body plating, and shields were no longer needed.

Chapter Eight

Thomas is probably quoting from a book—*The Art of War*—which may still be found today more than 2,000 years after it was written by a Chinese general named Sun Tzu, who lived hundreds of years before Christ was born.

Chapter Nine

While the concept of **reinforced bows** was definitely unusual to English archers during Thomas' time, other cultures—as far back as the ancient Egyptians—had experimented with bronze or bone plating to add strength to wood.

Chapter Twelve

The isle of the Celts is known today as Ireland.

The earliest known records of **Druids** come from the 3rd century B.C., and according to the Roman general Julius Caesar (who is the principal source of today's information on Druids), this group of men studied ancient verse, natural philosophy, astronomy, and the lore of the gods. The principal doctrine of the Druids was that souls passed at death from one person to another.

Druids offered human sacrifices for those who were in danger of death in battle or who were gravely ill.

The Druids were suppressed in ancient Britain by the Roman conquerors in the first century A.D. If indeed the cult survived, it must have remained as secret as it was during Thomas' time.

Today, followers of the Druid cult may still be found in England worshiping the ancient ruins of Stonehenge at certain times of the year.

Chapter Sixteen

The battle tactic which Thomas used to conquer a larger force was not new. Readers today may find in his book *The Art of War* the same tactic used more than 2,000 years ago by the Chinese military genius Sun Tzu.

Chapters Twenty-Five and Twenty-Six

For hundreds of years before Thomas' time, it had been commonly accepted that God would judge the criminally accused through **trial by ordeal** or by battle. In trial by ordeal, the defendant was made to undergo a severe physical test, such as burning or drowning. In trial by battle, the defendant faced his accuser in combat, usually with blunt weapons; the loser would be judged guilty and would often be hanged as a result.

In the year A.D. 1215 trial by ordeal was officially banished by the church. It would not be strange, however, for the people of Magnus to accept a self-imposed trial by ordeal or its deemed judgment, especially the one dramatically proposed by Thomas. Superstition was never very far away from the people, and trial by ordeal always promised great entertainment.

Chapter Twenty-Eight
Caltrops were four-pronged spikes, much like the modern-day "jacks" (except much sharper) of the game sometimes played by children with a ball and jacks.

The British Museum in London has caltrops on exhibit, remnants of the ones used—as Thomas mentions—by Roman soldiers to break up cavalry charges.

Chapter Twenty-Nine
Yew trees are found throughout the Northern Hemisphere. All but the red fruit of the plant is poisonous to humans. Symptoms of poisoning include nausea, giddiness and weakness, followed by convulsions, shock, coma, and death.

Poison ingested in smoke from the yew tree, especially concentrated in the narrow upward tunnel leading into the belfry may well have caused the "supernatural" daytime appearance and death of the bats—especially since low concentrations could harm the smaller mammals—in chapters 23 and 27.

There is, however, another possibility, one which has interesting implications perhaps unknown to Thomas. The *oleander* or *Jericho Rose,* a shrub which normally favors hot, southern climates, also releases a poisonous smoke when burned.